SLURRY

Josh Boldt

This is a work of fiction. Names, characters, businesses, places, events and incidents are either the products of the author's imagination or used in a fictitious manner. Any resemblance to actual persons, living or dead, or actual events is purely coincidental.

Copyright © 2020 Josh Boldt
www.joshboldt.com

All rights reserved. No part of this book may be reproduced or used in any manner without permission of the copyright owner except for the use of quotations in a book review.

First paperback edition October 2020
Brown Hound Publishing
Lexington, KY

Cover art by Brown Hound Publishing

PRINT ISBN 978-1-7359541-0-3
EBOOK ISBN 978-1-7359541-1-0

SLURRY

Josh Boldt

1

"This is the last place we saw her."

Debra Taylor choked back a sob, but the emotions overflowed from her eyes. She dabbed at her cheeks with the balled Kleenex in her right hand, the tissue black with mascara and damp from tears.

"She went in that door and disappeared," Debra continued, nodding at the rundown mobile home in front of them. "I'll never forget the way she looked back at me with that hateful glare in her eyes. What did we do to deserve this? We've been nothing but good to her. Nothing but good. And she left us for that awful life. I would have never let her go if I thought it would be the last time we'd see her."

The sobbing resumed and this time she could not suppress it. She turned to her husband, Elroy, and sunk her head against his chest. Her shoulders shook with grief. He wrapped his arm around her and continued telling the story where she left off.

"That good-for-nothing boyfriend of hers," said Elroy.

"He's the one that turned her on to the pills. Our little girl was the nicest sixteen-year-old kid around till she got mixed up with him and his crowd. It was like night and day when she started on the drugs. We lost her."

Cal Tyson listened as he scanned the trailer park for clues. What was he looking for? Signs of a struggle? A witness maybe?

"This is her boyfriend's trailer?" Cal asked. He thumbed at the mobile home twenty feet away. "The place you dropped her off on the night of her disappearance?"

"Oh, we didn't drop her off. We followed her here," Elroy answered. "I can't get around so good anymore on account of this busted up leg, so I had to drive." Elroy motioned down at his left leg which hung useless below him. He stood firmly on the right leg, supporting himself on a wooden cane with a black rubber cap on the bottom.

"Right. She was on foot then?"

"She was. As you know, we just live on the other side of the park. No more than a mile from here. She lit out after the argument and said she was going to Eddie's place." He shook his head and stared at the ground as he spoke. "Well, of course, we knew what that meant. She was going to get high. I wasn't about to stand by and let her do it. Not as long as I have a breath left in me. We ain't giving up on our little girl."

Cal nodded and waited for the man to continue.

"I got my cane and headed for the Buick. Debra was right behind me getting into the passenger side." Elroy patted his wife's shoulder and rubbed it to soothe her. "Willa was walking fast, but we caught up to her in the car. Her mother was hollering out the window for her to come back while I drove. But she was a brick wall. She wasn't having any of it. Just kept on walking without even looking back at us."

The girl's mother continued to cry quietly against her husband's chest. She spoke with a muffled voice through the tears. "I tried to convince her," said Debra. "We should have taken her away from here. We wanted to, but where would we go? Hazard's the biggest city around here and it's an hour away. We can't get too far from the mines or Elroy can't work. Oh, I wanted to take her out of here so bad, but we couldn't. If I had known…"

"That's right. We could only do so much, honey," Elroy comforted her. Then he continued talking to Cal. "Ever since my knee went out, I have to take what work I can get. Twenty years in the mines and I lost everything in one day when I lost my knee. At least they let me help out in the office now, but the salary I make doesn't compare. We used to be living good, but not anymore. Not anymore."

Elroy stared into the distance as he spoke. His voice trailed off, and his eyes focused somewhere far away into the hills of Eastern Kentucky.

Cal figured Elroy to be no more than fifty-five years old, but his eyes carried a look of exhaustion that could only come from a lifetime of struggle and disappointment.

"Can you tell me any more about the boyfriend?" Cal asked. "How old is he? Does he have any family around here?"

"Let's see. He was nineteen when they met. Three years older than her. They've been off and on for about three years now. So that makes him about twenty-one, twenty-two," Elroy answered. "As for family, I remember Willa saying he had an uncle out in the hills somewhere, but I can't say where. That's all I ever heard about Eddie's family.

He was an outsider and a troublemaker around here. The trailer park hasn't been the same since he moved in and brought the rough element with him."

"Rough element?" Cal asked.

"All the drugs and whatnot. We never had it around here before. This was a quiet place where people looked out for each other. The drugs have ruined all that. Now we've got people cruising through here at all hours. And the break-ins. I sleep with a loaded shotgun by the bed now. You can't trust these pillheads. They'd just as soon stick a knife in you as talk to you."

"I see. And Willa ran with that crew?"

"Not exactly. She mostly just went where Eddie went. Once she got started on the pills, she ended up with all the rest of the deadbeats. But even then she didn't like a lot of those degenerates. She still had a brain and knew enough to keep away from the worst of the bunch. Course we did our best to steer her clear when we could."

"Sure, I understand," Cal assured them. He wondered how much Elroy and Debra really knew. More than likely Willa was in a lot deeper than she let on to her parents. And Cal knew when it comes to addicts, you can't trust anything that comes out of their mouths. He decided to refocus the interrogation on the facts.

"Let's talk about the night she disappeared. What day did you say it was?"

"It'll be two weeks ago tomorrow. July 21st."

"You haven't heard from her since?"

"No, we haven't and that's unlike her. Even toward the end when things started getting real bad, she never went more than a day or two without talking to us," said Elroy. "She might stay with Eddie for a night, but never more than that. I'm telling you, deep down she was a good girl. It was the drugs that scrambled up her mind. That and Eddie. He pulled her away from us."

"Do you have any idea where she might have gone? Did she ever mention having friends in other cities? Any places she talked about visiting?"

Elroy and his wife thought for a minute.

Debra answered, "Years ago before she got on the pills she used to have big plans for herself. She wanted to get out of here and make something of her life. We encouraged it, of course. She was too good for the holler. She had a chance."

Debra nearly began to cry again, but she collected herself and continued, "I used to dream when she was a kid that she might go to college someday. Sometimes we'd watch the Kentucky Wildcats play basketball on television and talk about what it would be like to live in a big city like Lexington."

"Lexington, eh? Do you think there's any chance she could be there?"

"It seems like a whole 'nother world away to me," the woman replied. "How would she get there? She's never even left Pine Mountain as far as I know."

Cal could see she was pondering the thought in her mind.

"But I guess if there was any city she'd visit, Lexington would probably be it," said Debra. "It's the only place I've ever heard her talk about. Do you think she's there? Can you find her?"

"Ma'am, I don't know, but I will certainly try," Cal replied. "I don't want to get ahead of myself. First things first. I want to spend some time here. Get a lay of the land

and interview some of your neighbors."

The woman nodded and turned to look at her husband.

"We thank you for anything you can do, Mr. Tyson," said Elroy. "You came highly recommended from Debra's brother. Now, you know, we're people of little means, and we can't afford to—"

"I don't want you to worry about that at all," Cal cut him off. "Your brother-in-law is a friend of mine and I owe him one anyway."

"Well, we sure appreciate it. What can we do to help?"

"For now, I will welcome the extra bedroom you've offered. And," Cal added, "I wouldn't turn down a home-cooked meal."

"We can do that. The wife has a real gift in the kitchen," said Elroy.

He squeezed his wife's shoulder as he spoke. She looked up at him and mustered a smile.

"Good deal. I'm going to use this opportunity while Eddie is gone to do a little investigating. I'll meet you back at the trailer in an hour or so."

"Thank you, Mr. Tyson. We'll have dinner on the table."

"Much obliged. I'll see you then."

Elroy and his wife walked back to the Buick. Elroy opened the passenger door for his wife and shut it behind her. He pulled the back door open and laid his cane across the seat. He gripped the roof of the car and slowly shuffled to the front of the vehicle. He placed one hand on the headrest of the driver's seat and the other on the open door and carefully lowered himself behind the wheel. The whole way down his face contorted in a tight grimace. Once he reached the seat, he exhaled and rested a second before pulling his left leg into the vehicle by lifting it with

---

his hands. He started the car and backed out on the gravel road that led down the center lane of the trailer park.

The gravel popped and crackled as they drove away and left Cal standing alone by Eddie's trailer in the growing dusk.

2

The screen door hung off its hinges and banged against the aluminum frame of Eddie's trailer with each gust of the light breeze. The slamming door echoed through the trailer park and resounded off of the surrounding hills.

Sunshine Trailer Park occupied a depression of the earth—the locals call it a holler—that was sunk down in a valley near the base of Pine Mountain. The mobile home park was not far from Whitesburg, a small town on the Kentucky-Virginia state line just west of the Cumberland Gap.

The Appalachian Mountain range resides in Harlan County's backyard. The towering peaks that surround the county create a nest that cradles the people who live in it. Cal would soon discover that the barrier of mountains casts a shadow on the county. They block communications, cut off ties, and disrupt the region's ability to communicate with the outside world. Sound is captured and echoed back. Nothing gets out and nothing gets in.

The screen door slammed again. Metal on metal

reverberated through the hills.

Cal approached the trailer for a closer look. He saw a large dent in the frame below the handle, and the latch on the screen door was broken. The door had possibly been kicked in, which caused the frame to bow outward and it prevented the handle from latching to the jamb.

Cal stepped backward down the three stairs that led to the trailer door. He turned and circled the structure.

The trailer sat idle, tethered to a concrete slab. A dirty, white building with a green and yellow stripe around its entire perimeter. Attached to the front of the trailer was a set of wheels and a ball hitch for towing. Rust caked the hitch and weeds had grown up around it. The trailer had not been moved in some time.

As Cal circled the prefabricated aluminum structure, he noticed the windows were all covered with dirty screens except for one in the very back of the trailer. This sliding window looked bare without its screen. When Cal walked up to it, he spotted the displaced screen lying in the tall grass at the base of the concrete slab. Stubbed-out cigarette butts scattered around the screen. Some lay on the concrete slab and some had been tossed in the grass.

Cal bent over to examine the ground. He picked up one of the butts. It was a brown filter with the word Marlboro stenciled across it. The end of the filter stained brown with tar. He dropped it back in the grass and lifted the screen for a closer look.

The haphazard way that the screen lay just below the window indicated it had either fallen out or been removed intentionally and tossed aside. The grass under the window was pressed down and crushed under the weight of the screen, creating an impression in the thick undergrowth around it.

The grass around back of the trailer reached about halfway up Cal's calves. The weeds covered his shoes as he waded through the yard. He wondered if he should worry about ticks in the tall grass. Or even worse, copperheads. He carefully examined the ground in front of him before placing each footstep.

When the screen door slammed again, Cal almost jumped out of his skin. He spun around, watching for any sign that his presence had been noticed. He regained his composure and continued searching the grounds.

The sweet aroma of honeysuckle filled the air. It was the first week of August, and the late summer flowers were nearing the end of the blooming cycle. The light fragrance mixed with a more pungent scent that Cal couldn't quite identify. It reminded him of burnt motor oil. There were enough abandoned vehicles in the trailer park to explain the source of the second odor. Many of the cars sat on cinder blocks, devoid of tires, hoods raised, engines exposed to the elements.

The trailer backed up to thick woods. Directly behind the mobile home a white propane tank about the size of a small refrigerator perched on its stand. Just beyond the propane tank was a wire fence. The fence swelled inward under the weight of the wild behind it, fighting a losing battle against the trees and vines of the woods that sought to encroach on the property.

Cal ran his fingers across the propane tank. The metal was hot to the touch, having retained the heat from the afternoon sun. A flexible hose connected to a regulator on the tank. It led into the side of the trailer where it disappeared from sight.

The windows in the back of the trailer were all covered by dark red curtains. Cal tried to peer inside, but the cloth blocked any view of the interior.

His back faced the woods now and, behind him, Cal heard the sounds of nature rising to greet the approaching night. Cicadas hummed and crickets chirped. The woods came to life as the sun sank below the horizon.

Another noise grew ever-louder above the volume of the insect-filled woods. It was the sound of car wheels on gravel. Cal quickly began retracing his steps back to the front of the trailer.

By the time he reached the side of the building, the sound of rock music cut through the previously quiet trailer park.

The Scorpions "No One Like You" grew louder and louder until Cal could hear every word. Just as he was about to step onto the main road of the trailer park, a black Trans Am whipped around the corner and skidded to a halt in front of Eddie's trailer. Cal jumped sideways to avoid the vehicle as it lurched into the parking space.

Before Cal could react, Eddie was out of the car and charging toward him.

"What in the hell do you think you're doing, pal? This is private property."

Cal knew he would have to talk with Eddie eventually. Now was as good a time as any.

"Actually I was looking for you," he replied.

A look of confusion spread across Eddie's face. He stopped advancing, but he still blocked the exit of the trailer pad. He stood his ground, challenging Cal with wild eyes and a puffed out chest. He wore a pair of tight blue jeans and a black tank top. His skin carried a dark tan and his chin-length black hair was greased back over his forehead. His cheekbones were strong and dusted by a coat of thick, dark stubble. Eddie's lean muscles bulged under his close-fitting tank top. As he spoke he gestured toward Cal with a half-empty bottle of Budweiser in his left hand.

"That so? Well, you found me. Now start talking before I wrap this beer bottle around your head."

Eddie sneered as he spoke. He had obviously been drinking and had a look in his eyes like he wanted to blow off some steam at someone else's expense.

Cal raised his hands in front of him and took a step backward before answering.

"Easy, man. Don't worry. I'm not looking for any trouble. Just here to help."

"Who says I need any help?"

"It's not so much you as it is someone you know," Cal answered. "I'm trying to find Willa Taylor."

Eddie's eyes darted from side to side quickly. He blinked. "She ain't here."

"I know. I'm a friend of her parents and they asked me to help look for her."

"Goddamn it, I already told Elroy I don't know where she is. She ran off on me the same as everybody else. Maybe he shouldn't have tried so hard to keep up with her."

That's interesting, Cal thought. He pushed for more details.

"What do you mean by that?"

"I mean he and Debra never let Willa breathe. He liked to drive her crazy with all the rules and check-ins she had to do. In case he don't know, Willa's a grown woman and she can go wherever the hell she wants whenever the hell she wants."

"And with whomever she wants, right?" said Cal.

"You're damn right she can," said Eddie. He pointed the bottle of Bud at Cal to emphasize his point.

In his drunken state of mind, Eddie had gotten caught up in the moment and forgotten who he was talking to and why. But he had a sudden moment of lucidity and remembered he was supposed to be suspicious of this stranger on his property who was asking him questions.

"What is this anyway? Who are you?"

"The name is Cal Tyson. My specialty is finding people who don't want to be found."

"You're police?"

"No. Far from it. I'm a private investigator. The Taylors hired me."

"Whatever. I already told the police chief everything I know, so you can leave me alone."

"I aim to speak with him, too, but I often find traditional law enforcement can be a challenge in my line of work," said Cal.

"Alright then. Now you're speaking my language." Eddie smirked and drained the rest of his beer in one gulp. "Well, looks like I just hit dry land. I'm getting another. You want one?"

Eddie was already heading for the trailer as he spoke. He bounded up the three stairs and grabbed the broken screen door. He swung it open and stuck his key in the deadbolt lock. With his hand on the door knob, he looked back at Cal.

Might as well take advantage of this opportunity to learn more about Eddie. One beer and then get out of here. Eddie was the kind of guy who had a mean streak in him once he crossed a certain threshold.

"If you're offering, I believe I will have one. It's hot out here."

Eddie nodded. He pushed the door open and went inside the trailer, leaving it wide open behind him. The screen door swayed loosely in the breeze.

Cal heard Eddie open the refrigerator and remove two bottles of beer. The glass clinked together as he carried them across the room in one hand.

"Well, you coming or ain't you?" Eddie hollered from inside the trailer. "Quit letting the flies in!"

Cal wiped the sweat from his brow. He glanced around him at the other trailers in the park. It was almost dark outside now. Lights had switched on in most of the trailers. He could hear the faint hum of generators powering electricity. A window in the trailer across the street flickered with irregular light from a television set. He heard Pat Sajak introducing the night's contestants on Wheel of Fortune through the neighbor's open door.

Cal shook his head slowly. "Here we go again," he mumbled under his breath.

He stepped up the stairs to Eddie's trailer and went inside.

3

Cal walked through Eddie's door to find a small kitchen. Directly in front of him, a yellow formica countertop circled the room. On it, sat two cold Budweisers side-by-side, one of them already half-empty. Condensation glistened on the rim of the dark glass. It ran down the edges of the label and pooled on the counter at the bottle's base.

A thin layer of stained linoleum covered the floor of the kitchen. It peeled back from the wall at the floor's edges. The plastic flooring had yellowed from years of smoking, and it was pockmarked with tiny charred circles from dropped cigarettes.

Eddie fired up a smoke to go with his beer. The trailer filled with the exhaust expelled by his lungs. The smoky haze burned Cal's eyes. Eddie's trailer smelled like the break room of a mechanic's workshop.

A yellow bulb above the kitchen counter lit the small living area. Silhouettes of fly carcasses rested face up in the translucent plastic cover below the bulb.

Across the counter, the living room of the trailer

contained a plaid loveseat and a recliner with a broken footrest. Directly in front of the recliner sat a small television set topped by a pair of rabbit ear antennae. The brown shag carpet in the living room looked filthy even in the dim lighting. Laminated wood paneling lined the living room walls.

An ashtray on the end table near the recliner was filled to the brim and overflowing with cigarette butts. Ashes dusted the table and the brown carpet below the receptacle.

Cal took two steps into the trailer and reached for the Budweiser on the kitchen counter. The icy cold glass felt good on his hands. It was 85 degrees outside and it felt even hotter in the trailer. He tilted the beer back and swallowed the refreshing liquid.

"That's what I'm talking about. Nothing beats an ice cold brew at the end of the day," said Eddie. He stood in the middle of the kitchen, watching Cal as he drank.

Cal raised the beer in Eddie's direction. "No argument here. Thanks."

"Plenty more where that came from," Eddie replied. "Now what's all this business about Willa? You say the Taylors hired you to check up on me?"

Cal sensed the suspicion in Eddie's tone. The man was playing nice, but he was working an angle. Looking for more information.

"I wouldn't say that exactly. They're just concerned. It's no secret around here that you and Willa spent a lot of time together, so I wanted to start by talking to you."

"What, you think I hurt her or something?"

"I didn't say that at all."

"Good. Because I didn't. These other assholes in the trailer park will tell all kinds of lies about us. Have you talked to any of them yet?"

"Not yet. What do you think they will say?"

"No telling. All sorts of bullshit."

Cal took another swig of beer and waited to see if Eddie would elaborate.

"They'll tell you we fought a lot, for one."

"Did you?"

"Hey, buddy, that's not any of your goddamned business, is it?" Eddie's anger flashed up in an instant. His eyes glowed with a drunken fire as the muscles in his arms and chest tightened.

Eddie slammed the beer bottle on the counter and raised his hands to his forehead. He held them there for a second or two. He inhaled deeply. He exhaled a long breath and removed his hands. The fire in his eyes had dissipated. He picked up the burning cigarette from the ashtray on the counter and took a draw before continuing to speak.

"Yeah, sometimes we did. That's what happens when you love each other. You fight. She knew how to piss me off something awful."

"Do you think she ran away?"

"We've been together for three years. Since she was sixteen. I was her first, if you know what I mean." Eddie's face broke into a sinister smile. "She ain't running away from me. She's never been gone from the trailer park more than a day the whole time I've known her."

Cal thought about that for a minute. How could someone spend their entire life confined within a single square mile? There was so much more of the world out there to explore. He wondered if Willa had thought about life beyond the boundaries of the trailer park.

"Did she ever talk about leaving? Visiting friends or

family?"

"Are you kidding me? Every day, man. Most everyone in the park does. It's all pipe dreams. Ain't nobody going anywhere. We'll all be here till the day we die."

"Where did she say she'd go?"

"Where didn't she say? California, France, Canada, Disney World, the North goddamn Pole. She had a new place picked out for every day of the week."

"Would she ever do it?"

"That woman doesn't even know where France is, man. She probably thought she could hitchhike there," Eddie answered.

"What about Lexington? Did she ever talk about it?"

"Sure, once in a while. Everybody knows the University of Kentucky around here because of the basketball team. Hell, Lexington might as well be San Francisco as far as I'm concerned. Another world that I'll never see. But, yeah, she talked about it."

"Eddie, I need to ask you a question. I hope it doesn't make you mad. And let me assure you I don't care what you personally choose to do, but I need to know for the sake of Willa."

Cal paused, waiting for Eddie's reaction.

Eddie said nothing. He took a swallow of beer and stared back at Cal.

"Was Willa into drugs?" Cal asked.

Eddie squinted his eyes and looked away. He stared into the darkness at the back of the trailer. Seconds passed.

"Yeah," he finally grumbled while continuing to look away from Cal.

"What kind?"

"It ain't no secret around here."

"Humor me."

"Everybody likes pills. They make you feel real nice all day long."

"Willa was using pain pills? Swallowing them or snorting them?"

Eddie didn't respond.

Cal knew if she had progressed to crushing the pills and snorting the powder then the addiction had taken hold.

"Did you do the drugs together?" asked Cal.

"Do the drugs? Hell no, I don't do the drugs, man," said Eddie.

Cal was confused, and Eddie saw it in his eyes.

"But I know a lot of people who will pay a pretty penny for them," Eddie explained.

It clicked for Cal then. "I see. You sell the pills?"

"I think I've said all I'm gonna say about that, pal."

Cal nodded. "I get it. For the record, I'm not the police. Like I said, I don't care what you do. I'm just here to find a missing girl."

Eddie thought for a minute, then he said, "I told that woman not to sample the product. We had a pretty good thing going on. We were making some real cash till she went and started sneaking around on me, using up the product." Eddie shook his head as he spoke.

The pieces were coming together in Cal's mind. Willa and Eddie were selling pills, and that's how Willa got into the drugs.

"Do you mind my asking where you got the pills?" said Cal.

Eddie stared out the window, lost in a memory.

Cal asked him the question again.

Eddie whipped his head back around to look at Cal.

The fiery anger in his eyes returned in a flash. He raised his finger and pointed directly at Cal's chest.

"If you run and tell the cops, I swear to God I will put a bullet right here." He poked Cal's sternum for emphasis as he spoke.

Cal could smell the sour odor of stale cigarettes on Eddie's breath. That and the oily scent of pomade from his hair. Cal didn't break eye contact with Eddie. He reached for the Budweiser to his right, raised the bottle, and finished it off.

Eddie shook his head. He took a step back and relaxed again. "How bout another beer, guy?"

He reached into the fridge and produced another round of brews. Eddie's sharp mood swings made Cal uncomfortable.

"No, I think I'm good for tonight. I appreciate the cold one."

"You planning to stay in town long?" Eddie's eyes narrowed as he asked the question.

"As long as I need to."

"Alright then. You come down here and find me. We'll drink another beer and I'll show you around."

Cal again sensed Eddie's suspicion. Eddie barely bothered to conceal his disdain for Cal's questions. The forced smile and pseudo-friendly demeanor was a cover up. Eddie's offer to show Cal around was nothing more than an attempt to keep him close. He was slick. Then again, most addicts are. Cal wasn't so sure he bought Eddie's story about not using the drugs he sold.

"I just might do that."

Cal set the empty bottle on the yellow counter. The trailer door still hung wide open behind him. He pushed through the swinging screen and stepped out into the night.

The whole way back to the Taylors' place, Cal heard Eddie's broken screen door slamming against its metal frame in the darkness.

Down in the valley of Eastern Kentucky the sky gets dark early. The sun can sink below the mountains before dinner, and even the longer days of summer come with less daylight than in the city.

It was only about 7:30 p.m. when Cal returned to Elroy's and Debra's mobile home, but darkness had already come to the Sunshine Trailer Park.

Even in the 80 degree heat, the door to the Taylors' place was propped open. Like most others in the park they relied on a screen door to ventilate the trailer, only using the generator-powered air conditioning when absolutely necessary.

Cal heard the familiar sounds of dinner being prepared as he approached the driveway. Pots stirring on the stovetop, water running in the sink, a knife chopping on a wooden cutting board.

The smell of rendered fat wafted through the open screen. Grease and spices hung heavy in the air around the trailer and filled the yard with the scent of country cooking.

Elroy sat in a La-Z-Boy recliner just inside the door of the trailer. The glint of a television screen flickered in his eyeglasses. His cane leaned against the table next to his chair. He saw Cal approaching and motioned for him to come on in.

"You're just in time. It's Debra's special fried chicken."

Cal swung the screen door open and stepped inside. The aroma of fried food smelled even stronger in the trailer. Delicious, but the confined space was almost too small for the big aroma. The kind of smell that lingers in the kitchen for days.

He nodded at Elroy and complimented Debra on the fragrance she was concocting in the kitchen.

"How bout a beer, Cal? I'm having one."

Before Cal could respond, Elroy hollered into the kitchen at Debra.

"Two Coors Lights please, honey!"

The trailer was a double-wide—bigger than most trailers—but the space still was not particularly large. Cal could see the kitchen from the living room where he stood next to Elroy. He watched as Debra wiped her hands on a towel and removed two beers from the refrigerator. She walked around the counter and handed each man a bottle. Then she returned to her cooking.

Cal twisted the cap off his beer and took a seat on the couch.

"Well, did you find any clues at Eddie's place?" Elroy asked.

"Not really anything to speak of. He came home not long after you left me there."

"So you met him then? How did that go?"

"I needed to meet him sooner or later. Figured I might

as well get it over with," Cal answered. "He seemed okay tonight, but my first impression of him is that he's hiding something. It also looks like he has a pretty bad temper."

"Sounds about right. What did he say?"

"He's paranoid about you. Thinks you are trying to check up on him."

"We are! That no good prick took our daughter away from us," Elroy shouted.

"Elroy!" Debra said from the kitchen.

"I'm sorry, honey, but I can't help it. He's a greaseball and I don't like him."

"There's something else," said Cal. He lowered his voice so only Elroy could hear him. "I don't really want to tell you this, but you need to know."

"Mm-hm," Elroy mumbled. It was the kind of response people give when they are curious about something but not quite sure they want to hear it.

"I asked him about the drugs."

Elroy didn't react. He watched Cal quietly. The television reflected in the lenses of his glasses.

"You were right. It's pain pills."

Elroy sighed deeply and dropped his chin. He stared at the coffee table for several seconds. The two men sat silently.

Debra stirred a pot of mashed potatoes in the kitchen. Her wooden spoon clanged against the side of the metal pot as she folded its starchy contents.

"What is the Taj Mahal?" said the television.

"Right you are," answered Alex Trebek.

"I wish those drugs were never invented," Elroy finally said. He raised the beer to his lips, but then lowered it again without taking a drink.

Cal stayed quiet. He stared blankly at the television, waiting for Final Jeopardy.

"Dinner is served. Come and get it!" Debra announced.

Elroy set down his beer and grabbed his cane. He positioned the cane directly in front of the recliner and leaned forward. Pressing all of his weight on the wooden support, he raised himself up from the chair and began shuffling toward the dining table.

Thunk. Slide. Thunk. Slide. The sound of his cane hitting the wooden floor with his dead leg dragging behind him.

The trailer sat about four feet above the ground. Beneath the plywood flooring, a hollow space separated the floor from the ground. A metal skirt surrounded the mobile home and hid the empty space from view, but it created a cavern between the trailer and the dirt, and that cavern projected sound like a drum. Elroy's cane thumped and echoed in the dead space below. An exaggerated, hollow sound like an actor's footsteps on a wooden stage in a small theater.

They ate Debra's fried chicken and tried not to discuss the topic that laid heavy on all their minds. Finally, Debra couldn't resist anymore. She had to know Cal's plan for finding Willa.

"So, what's next? Do you have any ideas? What are you going to do tomorrow?" she asked.

"Now, honey, let the man work. Your brother says he's good at what he does," Elroy interrupted.

"But I need to know! We're running out of time…"

"It's okay, Elroy. This is a tough time. I'm happy to share everything with you as it comes to me."

Cal reached across the table and patted Debra's hand.

"Don't worry, Debra. We're going to find Willa," he

assured her.

She fought back the tears that swelled in her eyes.

"First thing tomorrow morning I'm going to have a chat with the local police. We'll find out what they know, get a list of possible suspects. I want to see if they have any leads on the investigation."

"You'll find the police department near the river on the main drag in town," said Elroy. "I need to stop at the hardware store in the morning before work. You can follow me in if you want."

"That'll be fine. Thanks."

"Can you be ready by seven? Across the street from the police is a diner with the best french toast you've ever eaten."

Cal's ears perked up. He was a breakfast man.

"Now you're speaking my language. Works for me."

Elroy nodded. He speared another piece of fried chicken and dragged it from the serving platter to his plate.

After dinner, the three sat together in the living room with the television providing background noise. They sipped Coors Light and talked about how things have changed in town with the coal industry waning.

Elroy and Debra explained that layoffs had sent the local economy into a tailspin. The unemployment rate in Harlan County was the highest it had been in a generation.

"When people don't work, they get restless. It's a recipe for trouble," said Elroy. "You get all these young people who are in the prime of their lives and they have nothing to do but sit around all day. They're bored. Most of them actually want to work. They'd love to contribute, but there just aren't any paying positions within a hundred miles of here."

Cal listened and nodded to confirm that he understood.

"Most of these kids aren't lazy. They work hard when there's work to be done. I mean, it's bad. If the Dairy Queen has a job opening, they get a hundred applications. And these are grown adults. Working for minimum wage! It's a damn shame."

"People who formerly worked in the mines?" asked Cal.

"Yeah, and they're used to making a decent living. Miners make the best blue collar wage in Eastern Kentucky. People around here would kill for a job in the mines if they could get it. A man can take care of his whole family on a miner's salary, but the work is drying up."

"What's causing the layoffs?"

"We don't know all the details. You hear bits and pieces. Lots of protests against mountaintop removal, for one. The rest of the country doesn't respect our vocation anymore. We keep their lights on for over a hundred years and they turn ours out the minute they lose interest."

"Isn't it true, though, that mining has all but destroyed the natural landscape around here?" asked Cal. "It can't be a good long-term strategy to strip the land of all its resources, can it?"

"Look, the coal mines have put food on my table for thirty years. I can never forget that. But I'm also not blind. I see the strip mining and the slurry ponds. What we do isn't good for the earth—I can admit that. But, shit. How can we worry about that when we can't feed our babies? A man will do a lot of things he's not morally thrilled about when his daughter needs formula and diapers."

"I hear that," Cal responded. "It's almost like there's no right answer."

"Bingo. You hurt the environment or you hurt your family. Take your pick."

Cal was familiar with the growing outcry against strip mining and mountaintop removal. Being from Lexington—Kentucky's second largest city—his daily life was pretty far removed from the economic realities of the hills of Eastern Kentucky. But he had heard plenty of protests by the Sierra Club and other environmental groups. He mostly agreed with moving away from coal-powered energy toward a cleaner source, but it's hard to hold that conviction when you are sitting in the living room of a man who made his living from the very profession you are lobbying against. He did not envy Elroy's moral and economic quandary.

"And the fracking. Don't forget about the fracking," said Debra. She had been listening quietly up until this point.

"Yeah, everyone's big on the natural gas nowadays," said Elroy. "Since it burns cleaner and creates less air pollution. A lot of the big energy companies are shifting resources away from coal and into natural gas. That's no good for us either."

"I've heard about that," answered Cal. "And the government seems to be more supportive of fracking, too."

"These big companies, they go where the money is. If the feds are subsidizing an energy source, well, that's where the fat cats concentrate their time and money. Coal is the red-headed stepchild now. Nobody wants to be seen supporting coal because it's not in fashion anymore."

"But isn't fracking even worse for the environment in

some ways? I've heard about the earthquakes and polluted water sources."

"My sister in Pennsylvania said she can light her drinking water on fire! The water that comes right out of her tap from the city," said Debra. "She lives on the Marcellus Shale and as soon as they started shooting chemicals into the ground, all hell broke loose up there."

"That's right," Elroy confirmed. "But nobody in the news talks about that. They're still picking on all of us who work in the coal industry."

The room became silent for a few minutes. The three stared blankly at the television set and sipped their beers. An oscillating fan hummed atop the kitchen counter. It rotated from side to side, blowing a stream of cool air across the room as it moved. Crickets chirped outside the trailer.

"Yeah, if I had it to do over again, I'd get into solar panels," said Elroy finally. "That's the future. The cleanest energy there is. The problem is the initial investment. It takes people five or ten years to start seeing a return on their money and most people don't think that far ahead. The government sure as hell doesn't. God forbid a senator might not get re-elected because he started the ball rolling on a long-term strategy that might save us all." Elroy shook his head softly and tapped his index finger on the end table to his right. "Yep, solar panels. That's what I should have done," he continued. "I'd be living the high life now. We'd be out of the trailer park. Debra would be driving a nice car. And Willa would have...she would have..." Elroy couldn't finish the sentence. He just trailed off into silence.

Debra stood up and walked over to Elroy. She put her hand on his shoulder.

"Let's go to bed, honey," said Debra. She helped him stand up from the chair and the two shuffled toward the back of the trailer.

"Cal, you help yourself to anything. Your bed is made and I left a clean towel in the bathroom for you," Debra said over her shoulder.

"Thank you. See you in the morning."

"Good night. We'll be back at it tomorrow bright and early." Elroy was trying his best to sound positive, but the tone in his voice betrayed the exhaustion of his spirit.

Cal watched as the two entered the bedroom and closed the door behind them. He switched out the light on the end table, set his empty beer bottle in the trash can, and retired to his bedroom where he would sleep in the bed of the missing teenage girl he came to find.

5

The morning sky streaked pink over Pine Mountain. Cal sat in his MG waiting for Elroy to lead him into town. When the trailer door swung open he glanced at his watch and saw it was 7:00 a.m. sharp.

Elroy's cane exited the door first and then his body slowly shuffled out behind the wooden stick. He stopped on the stoop and gathered his strength to descend the short ramp in front of him. Leaning on the railing, he raised his head and took a deep breath of fresh mountain air. He surveyed the trailer park like a general on a battlefield, part prideful and part vigilant.

Debra kissed Elroy on the cheek and waved to Cal.

"You boys be careful today. See you tonight!"

She watched with concern as Elroy navigated the handicap ramp they installed when he had the accident.

When Elroy reached the Buick, he opened the door and hollered back at Cal. "Just follow me and I'll point out the turn that will take you to the police station and the diner."

Cal gave Elroy a thumbs up and then started his engine.

They cruised along country roads for a few miles until they eventually hit Highway 931, which would lead them all the way into town.

The highway followed the ridge line to the right. The mountains of Appalachia loomed in the distance, overlooking the valley to the west. Farm land lined the left side of the highway. Rolling green hills and row after row of ripening tobacco plants. Cows grazed in the morning light, their tails flicking erratically to fend off the biting flies that had already begun gathering in the rising heat.

Elroy and Cal passed barn after barn. To Cal, everything looked the same. One tobacco field and then another tobacco field. A green tractor puttering across an empty expanse of wide open land. Hay bales neatly stacked in rows as far back as the eye could see. Using a farm as a geographical landmark would be like trying to use a single tree to navigate in the woods. Nothing distinguished one from the next. Cal struggled to remember what he had seen. He searched for visual cues to mentally record the route he was driving in order to find his way back later. Up ahead, Elroy's Buick drove onward.

As he drove, Cal craned his neck to see the peaks to his right. The hills that held the black diamonds, the keys to the local economy. He remembered Elroy's words from the night before. These mountains contained the riches that, in times past, could provide jobs to the entire state of Kentucky. Good jobs that a man could raise a family on, a middle class wage.

In those glory days coal ran the entire country. Elroy had informed Cal with pride that much of the electricity that powered the modern world passed through these hills back then.

But the days of prosperity were drawing to a close in this region. Coal power was no longer in fashion. Burning coal created pollution, strip mining wrecked the landscape, and the coal miners themselves suffered terrible health risks. It was a dirty, dangerous business for both the miners and for the world that relied on their product.

The topic of energy had lately become a hot political issue with both sides attacking the other. Small towns like this one in the heart of Appalachian coal country were being ripped apart in the middle.

Cal knew enough about the political divide to know there was no clear winner. The argument required far more nuance than either side would entertain. On the one hand, you had a pollutant that wreaked havoc on the environment and threatened the lives of the very people the industry employed. On the other hand were the economies propped up by the industry. The families who depended on coal to support themselves. The small towns that had nothing if not for the jobs provided by the coal companies. It was a catch-22. Impossible for both sides to win, no clear path to compromise.

Up ahead, Elroy stuck his hand out the window and pointed left at the approaching intersection. Cal put on his turn signal and braked as he prepared to follow Elroy's directions. He flicked his headlights at Elroy to thank him and watched as the Buick continued on up the road, around the bend out of sight.

French toast sounded pretty good to Cal's growling stomach, but first he wanted to stop by the police station. It never hurt to alert the local authorities before starting an investigation in town.

"What can we do ya for?"

The police officer addressed Cal from his desk. He allowed the top of his newspaper to droop so he could see over the folded edge. He watched Cal close the front door of the police station slowly, the glass door behind him gliding inward on its pneumatic hinge.

Cal didn't answer just yet. He stood in the entryway for a moment, getting his bearings. He saw the man who had spoken. A police officer with dark hair, graying on the sides. The man's newspaper covered the lower half of his face. Piercing blue eyes. His short-sleeved uniform exposed a pair of tanned and muscular forearms.

"I say, how can we help you, fella," the officer repeated when Cal didn't answer him.

Cal walked up to the front desk where the officer sat. He could see the officer's whole face now. A bushy, but perfectly trimmed mustache covered the man's upper lip. Dark, with wisps of gray intermingled throughout. It jumped and shook as the officer moved his mouth.

"Is the chief around?" Cal asked.

The officer pursed his lips slightly. The mustache arched and bent in the middle. He sniffed and returned his gaze to the newspaper.

Cal waited a few seconds for the man to respond. He watched the blue eyes scan the paper, reading the headlines.

"I would like to speak with the chief, if he's available," Cal tried again.

The officer pulled his attention from the newspaper and looked back at Cal. "Might be," was all he said.

"Would you check please?" Cal said.

The man slowly closed his newspaper and then folded it in half. He tossed it on the desk in front of him, then he sat up in the chair and placed his hands on the desk. "You ain't from around here, are you?"

"Lexington."

"Yeah, that's what I figured. A city boy."

Cal hardly considered Lexington, Kentucky to be the big city, but he wasn't about to argue with this police officer on his home turf.

"I guess so," Cal replied.

"I knew as soon as I saw that car you pulled up in," the officer continued. "Ain't many convertibles around these parts."

"Yep, you got me. I see why they made you a cop."

The man squinted his eyes. He squeezed a meaty fist and popped all the knuckles in his hand with one motion.

"What are you wanting, city boy?"

"I'm wanting to speak with the police chief like I already told you."

"Well, you've been speaking with him for five minutes. Get on with it."

"You're the chief?" Cal was surprised. "At the front desk?"

"We aren't exactly a huge staff around here. This town only has a couple thousand people in case you haven't noticed."

Cal had not anticipated such a minimal police presence, but it made sense that a small town would have a limited amount of tax revenue to pay its law enforcement. For all he knew, the chief was the only officer on duty at that moment. Better rein it in and be a little more friendly.

"I imagine it's not easy to police all this rural country with only a few of you. Must keep you guys pretty busy," he said.

"Yes, in some ways, fewer people in a town makes it even harder to police 'em," the chief answered. "They get so spread out across the hollers and god knows whatall they're doing out there. We can't keep an eye on everything like they can in the city."

Cal nodded. He hadn't thought of that challenge.

"Hell, half of them don't even see their nearest neighbor but once a week," said the chief. "And for a lot of them even once a week is too often."

"People keep to themselves around here then?"

"Some do. And the rest can't leave each other alone."

Cal laughed and the chief also smiled. His blue eyes lit up and his face tightened across his sharp jawline as he smiled, causing the mustache to spread.

"I guess I had better introduce myself," Cal said, still smiling slightly.

"I guess you'd better. Seems like you aren't going to leave me alone until you do." The chief's grin faded quickly.

"I'm a friend of Elroy Taylor's. Just down visiting. He helped me find your police station this morning. My name's Cal Tyson."

All traces of the chief's smile vanished. His eyes clouded over and he dropped his chin slightly. "Damn shame what's happening in that trailer park. Damn shame."

"They are pretty torn up about Willa's disappearance. That's why I am in town actually," Cal continued cautiously. "I work as a private detective up in Lexington. I'm hoping to be an extra set of hands. Maybe I can help with the search."

The chief stared at Cal without blinking. His eyes looked right into Cal's, right through him. "Should have known," was all he said. He picked his newspaper back up and pretended to read it.

"Hang on a minute, chief. I know it sounds like I'm here to second-guess you, but I assure you I'm not. I want to help."

The chief didn't even look up. He kept scanning the paper with his blue eyes.

Cal realized he was wasting his time. No sense pushing it just yet.

"If it means anything to you, I'm only here because of Elroy's brother-in-law. This is a personal favor to him. I'm not making a dime from the Taylor family."

"Down from the big city to help out the poor country folk who don't know any better. You're a real hero, pal. Now beat it."

"Hey, I get it, man. I'll stay out of your way," Cal said. "Here's my card, just in case you change your mind." Cal slid the business card across the desk. "At some point, I would like to have a real conversation with you about Willa Taylor's kidnapping."

The chief looked up. "Kidnapping? Who said anything about kidnapping? Willa Taylor is a grown woman. She can go anywhere she wants with whomever she wants. I know Elroy is broke up about it, but what am I supposed to do, track her down to tell her her parents miss her? She knows that and it hasn't changed her mind yet."

"So you think she left on her own free will?"

"This ain't a town hall meeting, bud. Now I already asked you to leave once. Don't make me ask again."

"Okay, I'm going." Cal raised his hands and began

backing away. As he pushed open the door, he glanced back over his shoulder and waved at the chief. "Hope to talk to you soon."

"That makes one of us," the chief muttered under his breath as the door slammed shut behind Cal.

Standing in the parking lot of the police department, Cal checked his watch. Barely sunrise on his first day in town, and he had already made quite an impression.

He wasn't surprised to discover the local police would not be his biggest fans. That was common in his line of work, especially in small towns outside of Lexington and Louisville. Small town law enforcement generally does not take kindly to interference from outsiders, especially not if they were from the "big city."

Searching for Willa in unknown territory was bad enough. Add to that a combative police force, and Cal's hope of finding the woman became nearly impossible. She could be anywhere in this backcountry wilderness. How could he even know where to start searching? Was she hunkered down snorting pills in some flop house? Had she run off to the surrounding woods to live with a biker gang? Or maybe neither. Maybe she had just escaped the drug world all together and vanished to Lexington without telling anyone.

Cal had no way of knowing and no leads. He had to start making some connections in town. Expand his network beyond the trailer park. Maybe someone had seen Willa or had an idea of her whereabouts. So far, no one knew anything, or at least no one was talking. But there had to be one person around here with information who was willing to help.

Cal pulled his cell phone from his pocket. Searching for a signal. He raised the phone above his head, moved it from left to right. He walked to the far end of the parking lot and back again with the phone raised in the air. Nothing. The barrier of mountains blocked cell phone signals, rendering digital communication futile. The mountains surrounded him, cradling the town. They kept the area safe from outsiders but also insulated it and locked the town's inhabitants in.

With no cell phone service, Cal had no easy way to contact the outside world. No way to call back to Lexington or reach beyond the boundaries in front of him. He was a captive to the mountains. He had to get used to the idea that, for the time being, he would return to an era that lacked many of the conveniences to which he had grown accustomed.

Cal slid the useless cell phone back in his pocket. He lowered his gaze from the foggy mountaintops and instead scanned his surroundings for the breakfast joint Elroy had recommended the night before.

Cal spotted the diner on the corner a block away. He would start by solving the one problem he could—his empty stomach.

6

While Cal stood in the parking lot of the police station searching for a cell phone signal, a navy blue Pontiac cruised down the main drag toward the center of town. As it approached the police station, a woman in the backseat spoke up.

"Hey, slow down a little."

"Why, you want us to drop you off? I bet they got a real nice spot for you in there," said the man driving the Pontiac. He looked in the rearview mirror, catching the eye of the woman who had spoken first. He bared his teeth and squinted his eyes in a vicious smile. The teeth were yellow and crooked, covered in a slimy film. White spittle filled both corners of his open mouth.

"Shut up, Luther. I'm sure the cops would love to hear all about you," she shot back. "In fact, why don't you drop me off so I can have a chat with them."

They were waiting at a stoplight directly in front of the police station now.

Luther eased the steering column into park. He placed his right arm on the back of the passenger seat and turned around to face the woman.

"I'm joking, I'm joking!" she said as he turned his body. "I wouldn't!" She pressed her back against the seat, squirming as far away from Luther as she could get in the small sedan.

Luther's eyes glowed with rage. They were bloodshot and dark like he hadn't been in daylight for some time, the pupils constricted into tiny points. Deep scars marked his face from scabs that had broken and only partially healed.

He stared at the woman for what felt like a minute before finally speaking. "You're goddamn right you're joking. If you ever even think about turning me into the police…"

The light turned green. The car next to them began moving. The guy in the passenger seat glanced around nervously. "Hey, uh, Luther, it's, um, green. The cops are right there, man. We better not draw attention."

Luther slowly turned back to face the road. The driver of the car behind them blew his horn. Luther stuck his arm out the window and raised his middle finger. Then, he shifted back to D and inched forward through the intersection.

As he drove, his eyes shifted back to the woman in the mirror. "I swear to god, Willa, do not fuck with me about that," he swore under his breath.

"I'm sorry, geez," she answered quietly from the backseat. Willa cowered down, doing her best to stay out of Luther's reach. She fidgeted with her seatbelt and stared at the floorboard. Dark sunglasses covered her eyes, blocking out the morning sun. Her body was tense. She hadn't slept. The pill she had been coasting on all night was wearing off. She could feel the world pressing in on her again. The pain she had been avoiding came rushing back all at once, like her whole body was one giant bee sting.

The mental pain hurt even worse. Memories of her parents, all the things she had done over the past few months haunted her. When she was high she could bury that mental pain deep down in her brain somewhere and forget about it. As the drug wore off, it all came flooding back. Guilt, regret, depression. The feelings washed over her. She felt like a surfer stuck under a wave, gasping for air but only gulping water as she thrashed against the current. She just wanted to curl up in bed and close her eyes. Pull a big, heavy blanket up to her chin and shut out the world in a long sleep.

Willa stared at Luther in the driver's seat. His jawline was covered with patches of curly, black hair that did little to hide the telltale signs of his addiction. The pasty, chapped skin. The splotchy, red scars. The dry, cracked lips. Luther looked like a pillhead.

Willa wondered if her own addiction was so obvious. She checked her arms and legs for scabs and scarring. Took a compact out of her purse and examined her face. A little thin, but not too bad. She lifted the sunglasses and saw the dark circles under her eyes. Her blue eyes were puffy and bloodshot like Luther's. They were a giveaway. She dropped the sunglasses back in place and shoved her compact into her purse.

"You better be sorry," Luther was saying as Willa drifted back to reality. "What are you rooting around in there for? You better not be taking another one without me. Matter of fact, give me another."

He reached his hand back behind the seat and opened it about six inches from Willa's face. His fingernails were long and dirty. His open palm rested in the air, waiting to be filled. The hand stunk of cigarettes, motor oil, and greasy pomade.

"What about me?" the guy in the passenger seat quickly added. Willa couldn't even remember that guy's name. Some other junkie hanging around Luther because he had a steady supply. Willa was getting sick of all these disgusting creeps Luther attracted.

Willa dug in her purse again until she found the bottle of pills Luther wanted. It rattled in her hand as she twisted off the top. She took out three pills. She placed two in Luther's hand. He gripped them quickly in a fist. He took one—quickly tossing it in his mouth and swallowing—and then passed the other one to the passenger creep. His hand stayed low, under the dashboard, out of sight of any watchful eyes in nearby cars.

The third pill Willa placed in her own mouth. She swished up enough saliva to swallow the pill and gulped it down. Her body began to relax immediately with the anticipation of the narcotic's effect. She receded back into the navy blue cloth seat, rolled her head to the left to watch the world pass by. The morning air felt cool as it flicked across her face from the open driver's window. She smelled the mountain mist in between wafts of smoke from Luther's burning cigarette.

Willa stared vacantly out her own window at the police station as they drove past. A man stood in the parking lot next to a silver convertible. He had his cell phone raised in the air, trying to find a signal. She watched as he moved the phone from side to side. The man with the silver convertible eventually shook his head and slid the phone back in his pocket.

Willa closed her eyes and waited for the pain to disappear.

Cal left his silver MG convertible parked at the police station. He crossed the street and walked to the diner for breakfast, following the scent of bacon and syrup, knowing these hole-in-the-wall country diners have the best home-cooked food money can buy. If the aroma was any indication, this place would fit the bill.

Red vinyl booths lined the front wall of the diner. The booths nestled up against a stretch of windows that overlooked the main drag of town. Cal grabbed a newspaper from the counter and chose a booth near the back of the restaurant.

Bright, blue sky painted the window next to Cal's booth. The vinyl seat, heated by the streaming sunshine, felt warm on his legs and back.

Outside, the small mountain town had come to life. Cal watched the street through his window as it filled with cars and people.

"Lucky you. You picked the diner with the best coffee in town."

Cal looked up to see a waitress standing next to his table. She held a steaming pot of black coffee poised above the white porcelain mug to Cal's right. She waited for him to give the signal. He nodded, and she began pouring.

"You act like I came here by accident," said Cal. "What makes you think I didn't plan out my breakfast joint?" he asked as she poured the coffee.

"Oh, just a guess I reckon." She stopped pouring the coffee and looked Cal over. "Never seen you around before, and something tells me you're a stranger in a strange land." She smiled as she spoke. Her accent was thick. Clearly a local. A country gal from the hills of Eastern Kentucky.

"Why does everyone keep saying that?" Cal asked. "Is there something about me that shouts foreigner?"

The waitress laughed. She set the coffee pot down on the table. Still smiling, she said, "That doesn't surprise me. We have a way around here. It's hard to explain, but you can just tell when somebody is different."

She was about thirty years old. Looked like she could have been prom queen in her prime but had a rough go in her twenties. Maybe had a kid, a tumultuous marriage. A decade on her feet working long hours. Tiny cracks creeped in around her eyes and mouth as she smiled, but she still had energy and vibrance. Her beauty was there somewhere buried beneath the waitress smock and coffee stains.

"I need to work on that I guess. Try not to be such a city boy," Cal laughed along with her.

"Does that mean you're planning on sticking around for a while?"

Cal thought for a moment. "Well, it's hard to say. You never know what the day might bring," he answered. Then he added, "I reckon." As he spoke he looked up and met her eyes with a wink.

"Now you're getting the hang of it." She broke the eye contact and glanced away momentarily. She reached for the menu and placed it in front of Cal. "Know what you want for breakfast?"

Cal ordered. He picked up the newspaper to read while he waited for his food.

"More Coal Jobs Cut" announced the headline on the paper's front page. The featured story explained that another round of layoffs had taken place at the Jefferson Mining Company nearby. Two dozen more men had lost their jobs. They joined the other unemployed coal miners who could no longer afford to pay mortgages or put food on the table for their families. According to the article, there were no jobs in the region that offered wages comparable to the salary a coal miner could earn. These men would soon be working in fast food or at grocery stores if they were lucky. If they were not so lucky they may get caught up in the region's other rapidly-growing industry: Narcotics.

It was a lose-lose situation for these men who would do anything to feed and shelter their kids. Once the lucrative coal jobs vanish, they have to figure out some other way to pay the bills. Even a good man can turn bad when he is forced to decide between providing for his family or breaking the law.

Cal turned the pages, browsing absentmindedly between sips of coffee. High school sports and coal seemed to be the major headlines around the region. On the back page of the newspaper a small advertisement caught Cal's eye.

Addicted?
We can help.
Save your life. Join The Farm.
777 Natural Way

The waitress reappeared carrying a tray laden with Cal's french toast, syrup, and bacon. Cal folded the newspaper and set it over to the side.

"Now this is one hundred percent pure maple syrup right here. None of that sugar water you get from the Waffle Hut down the road," the waitress said as she set the plate on the table.

"Smells delicious."

"Oh, it is."

She turned to walk away but before she could leave Cal said, "Hey, kind of a strange question for you. But since you're a local, maybe you can help me. Do you know anything about this place called The Farm?"

A split second of recognition flashed across the waitress's face. Her eyes widened slightly and her breath caught in her throat. She looked away. "No, uh, no, I'm not familiar with it."

Before Cal could respond she was gone. Around the counter and back into the kitchen.

Cal knew enough to know that was a cover-up. The waitress was hiding something. What did she know about The Farm, and why was she keeping it a secret?

He ate his breakfast to the classic country soundtrack of the jukebox. Patsy Cline, George Jones, Loretta Lynn.

The waitress did not return to his table.

When he finished eating, Cal approached the counter to

pay his bill. Another waitress smiled at him and took his cash. "Everything taste okay?" she asked.

"Yes, just fine. Thank you."

Cal looked over the woman's shoulder through the swinging double doors that led to the kitchen. Each time they swung open he searched for the first waitress. No sign of her.

"Say, what happened to the waitress who took my order?" Cal asked.

"Oh, I think she's on her break."

Cal paid his bill and exited the restaurant. As he began to cross the street and walk back to his car, he saw the first waitress around the side of the diner. She was sitting in a worn out chair between the back door and the grease dump, smoking a cigarette.

Cal turned and headed toward her. She saw him and hurriedly sucked down a draw from the cigarette, flicking it behind the dumpster as she exhaled the final breath of white smoke. She gathered up her apron and started to go back inside.

Cal picked up the pace and caught her before she could escape.

"Hey, hang on a sec," he said. "Did I say something wrong in there? Where did you go?" he asked.

She glanced around furtively, looking for a way out. "No, you're fine. It was just my smoke break is all."

Cal saw through her attempt at deflection.

"Was it because I mentioned The Farm? Is that what made you ditch me?" he laughed as he spoke, trying to lighten the mood.

She managed to crack a wan smile in response. "I don't really want to talk about it. It's not really something I share with anyone, let alone complete strangers."

"Have you been there?" Cal probed. This was the first possible lead he had encountered. He had to try.

She sighed. Took out her cigarette pack and lit another one before proceeding. "Yeah, I stayed at The Farm for a few months to get clean." She stared down at her shoes, fiddling with the drawstring on her apron. "I picked up a habit just like everyone else around here. Had to do something drastic or I would lose my kid."

"Pills?" Cal asked.

She nodded. "I hurt my shoulder carrying trays in there." She indicated toward the diner. "My doctor wrote a prescription for Lortab and I was off to the races. They don't tell you how good that stuff makes you feel." She took a draw from the cigarette and exhaled out the side of her mouth.

Cal waited for her to continue. He needed to learn more about The Farm. Maybe they had seen Willa out there.

The waitress stood still, quietly smoking her cigarette. The pungent odor from the grease trap mixed with the festering trash in the dumpster created a truly vile stench. Cal wondered why anyone would spend their precious fifteen minute break in this cesspool of garbage and fryer waste.

"What is it like out at The Farm?" he asked.

"It's…it's…" the waitress started to speak but stopped. She was going quiet on him again. She stubbed out the cigarette with her foot. "Listen, I have to go back in. Why do you want to know all this? Who are you anyway?" She was done talking. Cal sensed her suspicion of him. He was a stranger probing around in her personal life.

"I'm a friend. I am here to help the family of a girl who is caught up in that same mess you escaped." Cal put his hand gently on her shoulder. "I don't mean you any harm and I won't cause any trouble for you. Just looking for some help getting started."

She allowed Cal's hand to rest on her shoulder and raised her gaze to meet his. "You really don't want to get caught up in that place," she said. "You don't know what you're getting yourself into."

Cal squinted his eyes. "It sounds like I don't really have a choice. Maybe they can lead me to the missing girl."

The waitress took a deep breath and exhaled. "If you are going to The Farm, there are some things you need to know. Meet me at the coffee shop about a mile down the road at 2:00 p.m."

8

Paint peeled from the ceiling of the dank motel room. Yellowed and curling in strips, it hung above the bed, threatening to drop at any moment. Willa stared up at the paint strips wishing one would flake and fall into Luther's mouth as he lay snoring beside her.

A tiny metal chain on the fan rattled rhythmically as the rotors spun above the bed. Plaid curtains, pulled tightly across the window in a futile attempt to darken the room, did little to suppress the light that crept in around the sides of the window dressing. Ashtrays littered the counters and table. Jammed full of cigarette butts. The room stunk like stale beer and smoke. Discarded cans of Keystone Light scattered on the dresser and floor.

Willa sat up in bed. She leaned her thin shoulder blades against the wooden headboard. The mattress creaked as she shifted her weight. She had been lying in the dim light for an hour, trying to will herself back to sleep. Trying to ignore the pounding headache, the growing hangover that coursed through her body.

She looked at Luther. "Hey," she said, her voice cracking.

He continued to snore.

She poked him with her toe. "Hey, you awake?" she asked again louder.

Still no response from Luther.

She heard cars passing on the street outside their motel room. Her throat was parched. She searched around the room for something to drink. A half-empty beer sat on the nightstand to her right. She picked it up, sniffed it. A sickening smell of stale, warm beer. She set the beer back down. She took a deep breath, exhaled, and then swung her legs over the side of the bed. She placed her feet side by side on the dirty carpet. She sat there for a while, gathering the strength to stand, fighting the urge to lay back down.

Willa stood up and walked over to the sink. It was one of those motel rooms where the sink is outside of the bathroom. Dingy, pink countertop. She ran the water for a few seconds, then cupped her hands under the faucet. She raised her cupped hands to her mouth and drank, splashing the rest of the water on her face.

Her reflection stared back in the mirror. Mascara running down her cheeks. The face she saw reflected back looked tired and pale. She had lost more weight. She never did have much to lose anyway. She turned to the side. Lifted the t-shirt to her ribcage to see her thin waist. Hip bone sitting high above her cotton panties. She was getting too skinny.

She dropped the t-shirt back down to cover herself and wiped her face with a hand towel hanging by the sink. She walked back across the motel room to the door. Luther was still snoring on the bed.

Willa opened the door, flooding the room with sunlight. She stood in the open doorway and let the sun warm her body. Wearing only the t-shirt and panties for the whole world to see.

Luther sniffed loudly. "Close that goddamn door," he growled.

She looked back at him, but gave no response. Pulled the slide lock inward to catch the door and keep it from locking behind her, and stepped out on the second floor walkway.

She gripped the steel railing in front of her and leaned forward, observing the motel's parking lot.

The motel was built in the shape of a horseshoe with the parking lot in the middle. Willa could see the whole property from her second-floor catwalk.

Across the lot a maid's cart waited outside the open door of another room. It surprised Willa to know these rooms were ever cleaned. She and Luther had been staying there for a week and had never seen a maid or had anyone ask to change the sheets. Maybe Luther had told the front desk not to bother them. Or maybe they just slept too late to see the cleaning crew.

In the center of the parking lot was a small swimming pool, surrounded by a black iron fence. The pool was empty except for a deflated beach ball floating aimlessly in the water. Half a dozen lounge chairs with vinyl straps littered the deck in various degrees of recline.

The summer sun felt good on Willa's body. She looked up at the sun, felt it drying the last drops of tap water from her face.

A sun tan, that's what she needed. To lay by the pool for a few hours. Let the sun warm her and refresh her. Get a little color back in her face. Maybe she wouldn't even take a pill this afternoon. The sunshine was all she needed today. If she could just lay by the pool and feel the summer sun, she might be okay.

She would have to get a bathing suit and sunglasses. She organized the plan in her head like a checklist. The sunglasses she already had. They were in the room somewhere. Go in, get the sunglasses, put on some shorts and flip-flops. Then take some money from Luther's pants and go to Walmart to buy a bathing suit.

Having the plan helped her mind. It shook the cobwebs loose. Stick to the plan. No pill today. Get the sunglasses, go to Walmart.

She pushed the door open and entered the dark motel room. Her eyes temporarily flashed bright colors from staring up at the sun. They slowly adjusted to the dim light. The door banged closed on the slide lock behind her.

Luther was sitting up on the bed. He stared at the floor, smoking a cigarette butt he had found in an ashtray. He didn't even look up at her. "You showing your ass to the whole town?"

"I just wanted to feel the sunshine on my skin. It's a nice day."

"Well, put some fucking pants on next time."

Willa didn't respond. She picked up discarded clothes and tossed them aside, searching for her sunglasses. After a few moments, she said, "Have you seen my shades?"

Luther leaned over the nightstand. He held the bedside lamp in his hand. He was poised over the nightstand holding the lamp like it was a hammer, like he was about to smash a spider with it. "I don't know, honey, you came in here last night and threw everything everywhere. There's no telling where you put them."

He had cleared a spot on the nightstand, and he was blowing the ashes away to make a clean surface.

"Okay, but I need them. I need to go to Walmart," she said as she searched the room.

"Oh yeah? What you gonna do there?"

"Get a bathing suit."

"What do you need with a bathing suit?

"The sun, it felt so good on my face out there. I want to go down to the pool and lay out today."

"You want to swim in that nasty ass pool?"

"Not swim. I just want to lay on one of those patio chairs and get a sun tan."

"You gonna get you a sun tan, huh?"

"That's what I said," she snapped, getting frustrated with his patronizing questions.

"Shit, okay then. Go get you a sun tan." He set the lamp down on the nightstand and raised his hands to show he didn't want to argue with her.

"Here they are!" She picked up the sunglasses from under a rumpled shirt and slid them on her face. She walked over to the bed and sat down next to Luther. Realizing she couldn't see anything in the dark room, she raised the sunglasses up. Perched them on top of her blonde head. She put her hand on Luther's leg. She changed her tone abruptly. Her voice became sweet. "Can I have some money?" she asked.

"Here it comes. I knew you wanted something," Luther answered.

"Just a few dollars to get a bathing suit." Still using that sweet tone. "You know you want to see me in it anyway."

"You think you know how to work me, don't you?"

"Yes." She smiled at him with those sunglasses sitting up on her head.

Luther smiled back. "Go get my pants."

She found his pants laying on a chair next to the table. She reached in the pocket and pulled out a wad of cash. Took out a bill, shook the pants to straighten the legs.

"Here." She walked back to the bed with her arm outstretched, holding the pants.

Luther had hunched over the nightstand with the lamp in his hand again. Then she heard it. The sound of the lamp base grating against the nightstand. The pill breaking and crushing under its weight.

"Thanks, baby doll," he said.

Luther used his driver's license to sift the white powder and cut it into lines. Willa watched as he cut out three lines on the nightstand. He reached into his pants pocket and pulled out a dollar bill. Rolled it up tightly. Raised it to his nostril and snorted two of the white lines. He handed her the bill.

"I was thinking maybe, um, I was thinking I might not today." She spoke the words she had rehearsed on the balcony but didn't sound like she meant them. Her body wanted to do the line. She could feel the drip in the back of her throat as her sinuses prepared for the powder. So hard to resist when it was right there.

"You gonna turn down a beautiful thing like that? Sitting right there waiting for you to do it?" He still held the rolled up bill in his hand, his arm outstretched, offering it to her.

She took the bill. Looked at the white line. Fidgeted for a few seconds. "Can I just take one? One to swallow I mean? My nose is too stuffed to put more in there."

"It goes farther if we snort it."

"I don't want to right now. Can I just have a whole one?"

"Damn, woman. First the bathing suit and now this. You're costing me more than you're worth today." He shook a pill from the bottle and handed it to her.

"Thanks, baby." She palmed the pill and kissed him on the cheek.

"You ain't even gonna take it here with me? Stay in bed and give me some love for being so nice to you?"

"I need some water. My throat's too dry." She was already pulling on her shorts.

Luther watched sullenly as Willa slid on her flip flops, dropped the sunglasses back over her eyes, and left the motel room without saying another word.

Cal found the coffee shop easily enough. Only one street ran through town, so you couldn't miss much if you stayed on it.

Following the waitress's request, it was two in the afternoon when Cal walked through the door of the coffee shop. Clean and cozy. Leather chairs in one corner, wooden tables, standard coffee shop apparatus behind the counter, NPR-style music on the stereo. Aroma of freshly-ground beans. It looked, smelled, and sounded like any other coffee shop Cal had patronized in bigger cities.

He spotted the waitress at a table. She leaned back in her chair, watching him. Cal raised his head to acknowledge her. Ordered a coffee at the counter and carried it over to the table where the waitress sat. He pulled out a chair and joined her.

"Off work for the day?" he asked.

"Finally. I'm in there by five so we can start serving at six. We have an early crowd before the mines open."

"Ah, that is an early morning," said Cal. He was

thinking about how to explain his investigation to this woman. Could he tell her the truth, what he was really doing?

"Listen, I want to thank you for meeting me like this," he said. "I wasn't trying to pry in your business. It's just that you seem to know something about the subject matter of my work, and I could really use your help. As you noticed, I'm not exactly in my element. I'm an outsider trying to learn a new language."

Cal's frankness and formality brought a smile to the woman's face. She had changed out of her waitress uniform. Her hair was fixed and makeup reapplied since Cal had last seen her. A light summery perfume wafted across the table. Slightly floral with a touch of citrus, contrasting with the sharp acidity of the steaming coffee.

"Clearly," she replied. Her eyes lifted and shone when she smiled, lighting up her face.

"You know, I don't even know your name," said Cal after a few seconds of silence. "Mine is Cal. I'm from Lexington."

"Well, Cal from Lexington, I'm Penny. Penny Fairfax."

"Nice to meet you, Penny. I don't think I have ever known a Penny."

"Until now," she said.

"Until now."

They both smiled.

Penny said, "What are you doing down here in Pine Mountain, Cal from Lexington?"

Cal looked out the window and took a sip from his coffee, thinking about how to answer. Stick to the basics, tell her what she needs to know for now.

"I mentioned I am here to help a friend. Elroy Taylor.

His daughter disappeared a few weeks ago. They think she is caught up in drugs."

Penny nodded, her elbows resting on the table. Coffee mug raised just below her chin. She sipped from it occasionally as she listened to Cal.

"The problem, I guess, if we want to call it that, is the girl—Willa is her name—is an adult," said Cal. "She's nineteen. Not exactly a kidnapping case. Elroy and his wife really have no legal claim on her any more. Willa can go anywhere she wants with whomever she wants."

"Even if that means she's wrecking her life," Penny interjected.

"Exactly. And believe me, the police chief made that abundantly clear to me this morning."

"What do you mean?"

"He said there was no way they could force her to come home since she is legally old enough to make her own decisions."

"You mean you walked into the police station on your first day in town and told them how to do their job?"

"Well, not exactly. I guess I was hoping we could share information and work together," Cal answered. "Why, what would you have done?"

"Um, not that, for starters. You need an introduction to get the trust of locals. You can't just waltz in here and start telling people their business. Not if you want to make any friends, that is."

She had a point. Things operated differently around here. The community was more insular, harder to break into without a local connection to vouch for you.

"I'm starting to realize that now," Cal said.

"And if you think the *police* gave you a hard time,

wait until you roll up to The Farm and start asking questions. They just might run you out of town."

There was that mysterious caution about The Farm again. What was it about the place that made it so troubling? Cal wanted to ask how she knew so much about The Farm, but he didn't want to scare her off. He remembered Penny was hesitant to divulge too much about her personal experience.

"I think I need to pay a visit to the place despite your words of caution," he said. "They may have seen or heard from Willa."

"But you said yourself she's a grown adult and, even if you do find her, it's not like you can grab her and drag her home. Believe me, a drug addict will never change until they are ready. There is no forcing an addict to do anything they don't want to do. Especially if it involves getting clean."

"Maybe she wants to get clean but she needs help. If I can find her, I can at least tell her how much her family misses her. Take a shot at breaking her from the spell. Or maybe she is being held against her will. What if she's mixed up with a rough crew and she can't get free from them?"

"Don't get your hopes up. This isn't going to be some knight-in-shining-armor thing where you find her, say a few Bible verses, and suddenly she renounces narcotics and sees the light. It just doesn't work like that. Once you're addicted, you are always an addict for the rest of your life. You might stop using, but you never forget the high. You want it again, and you have to fight against relapse every day."

Cal fell silent. This woman clearly had experience with

addiction in a way he could not personally understand.

Penny sensed his deflated hopes. "What I said is true, but it doesn't mean you shouldn't try. I mean, I am proof it can work. At least give it a try. That's all you can do. Do your best to help her."

"That's the promise I made to her parents," said Cal. "And it's why I want to head out to The Farm this afternoon."

"Okay, I understand. You're probably right." Penny paused for a second to think. "If you are going, you need a story. There's no way you will get anywhere out there as a straight-laced square poking around in their business."

Cal considered her advice for a moment. He was no stranger to the element of disguise, having used it several times in past cases. He could play a part if it would lead to insider information. "You think I should pretend to be a recovering addict?"

"If you can pull it off. Have you ever taken an opiate?"

Cal had. Years ago, after a surgery, the doctor had prescribed a heavy dose of Vicodin with refills. By the time the refills ran out, Cal was reluctant to give up the euphoria that came with taking them. It took some serious restraint to fight the urge to track down an illegal source for the pills so he could continue to feel that comfortable numbness. He understood exactly how someone might develop an addiction to that feeling.

"Yes, I have," he responded.

Penny looked surprised by his answer. She seemed to respect him more knowing he wasn't as clean cut as he appeared. "That will help your story then. And you need different clothes. Stop at the Goodwill on your way out of town. Pick up some jeans and a flannel."

"Will do. Anything else I should know?"

"Don't talk too much. Don't go in there asking questions immediately. Build some trust before you ask for anything. They are big on communal effort out there. If you can prove you have something to offer they will be more likely to return the favor."

"I can handle that," said Cal. He was starting to get nervous about this plan. The way Penny described the place it sounded like prison.

"I realize I just met you, but considering what you are doing, I want to help," said Penny. "This girl, Willa, sounds a lot like me when I was her age. Maybe I can save her from the decade of shit I put myself through." Her voice trailed off as she spoke the last sentence. Her eyes shifted to the window and she stared into the parking lot.

"Thank you," said Cal. "You have been a big help already. I really appreciate it."

Penny broke her trance and looked back at Cal. "Good luck out there. I want to know how it goes. I feel like I'm part of the story now. Let me know if you learn more."

Willa flipped absentmindedly through the swimsuits on the rack at Walmart. Still wearing her sunglasses, she glanced up from the clothing rack occasionally, looking around the store to see if she recognized anyone.

It was sometime after lunch. She didn't have a watch or her phone so she wasn't really sure of the time. Not that it mattered anyway. She had nowhere to be other than the pool before the sun left.

The pill Luther had given her was in the front right pocket of her shorts. She could feel it in there when she brushed her hand across the outside of her pocket. A tiny little bump like a pimple on her thigh. Well over eight hours since she had taken one. Her body was starting to crave it. She couldn't go more than a few minutes without thinking about the little pill.

She shook her head and spoke softly to herself, "Not yet."

She grabbed a couple of two-piece bathing suits from the rack and headed for the dressing room.

"How many?" asked the dressing room attendant as Willa approached.

"Um, two."

"Ok, go on back," the woman said. "You know you're supposed to leave your underthings on when you try on swimsuits."

"I know," Willa said as she brushed passed the attendant.

She entered the dressing room and began taking off her clothes. She lifted the sunglasses off her eyes just long enough to raise her t-shirt above her head and then she let the sunglasses drop back in place. The bright fluorescent lighting was more than she could handle right now.

Once undressed, she stood facing the mirror. Nothing on but her underwear and sunglasses. She was skinny. She didn't remember ever being as skinny as she was now. The bones in her hips stuck out like two handles on either side of her waist. She touched them with her fingers, felt the sharp points of the protruding nobs just above her waistline.

She took the swimsuits off their hangers and tossed them on the bench in the dressing room. She grabbed the first pair of bottoms and held them out in front of her.

Balancing on one leg, she stepped into the tiny bikini bottoms and pulled them on over her panties. Then she stretched the bikini top around her chest and fastened it over her bra. She looked in the mirror. The bikini top was too tight. Her bra stuck out from underneath it. She couldn't get a good sense of how the suit would look.

Willa glanced around the dressing room, wondering if they had cameras installed to keep people from stealing. Was that even legal? Probably some creepy assistant manager in a back office watching her. If so, he was about to get a show. She took the bikini top off and then unfastened her bra. Surely she couldn't catch something from the bikini top. She refastened the bikini top on her bare skin. It fit much better now without the bra underneath.

Willa turned sideways in the mirror. Stared at her profile in the sharp, fluorescent lighting. Slim shoulders, thin waist, long, brown legs, and a nice round butt in the middle. She was too skinny, but at least she still had her butt. She snapped the elastic band on her waist and managed a little laugh. The swimsuit was a winner. Navy blue with green polka dots. Looked good with her dark sunglasses and sandy blonde hair.

She didn't even bother trying the other suit on. She wanted this one. Excited to wear her new suit at the pool, knowing it would feel good to be outside in the sunshine again—the first time she had felt excited about something in a long time.

Willa took off the swimsuit and got dressed. As she pulled on her shorts, the little pimple in her pocket again called her name. A rush of anxiety flooded her body. It started in her chest and shot down to her toes and back up to the top of her head. She shook with a cold shiver. Leaning in close to the mirror, she raised the sunglasses with one hand and looked into her eyes. Tiny beads of sweat formed on her forehead and lip. She wiped it away with her sleeve, grabbed the bathing suit, and left the dressing room.

"Ma'am, where is the other suit? You took two in there with you," the dressing room attendant called after Willa as she breezed past.

"Hmm? Oh. It's in there still. I didn't want it," Willa said over her shoulder. She was already halfway to the checkout lanes. She couldn't be in this store another minute.

Willa found an empty lane and placed the suit on the conveyor belt. She fumbled in her pocket for the $20 she had taken from Luther. Fished it out and tossed it up on the conveyor belt with the bathing suit. Her hands were shaking slightly now. The sunglasses did little to protect her from the world that pressed in on all sides. The beep beep beeping of the price scanner. Shopping carts slamming into the corral near the entrance. People talking all around her.

"Hello, did you hear me?" the checkout clerk said again, and Willa realized she was being addressed.

"I'm sorry. What did you say?"

"The swimsuit is $21.19. You only gave me $20."

Willa searched her pockets knowing she didn't have a penny more. Her fingers grazed the pain pill as she dug deep in her pocket. "I'm so sorry. I don't have anymore. That's all I have. I thought it was $19.99."

"Plus tax," the woman answered apologetically. She seemed genuinely sorry for the girl's predicament. "You mean you don't have another dollar at all?"

"I really don't. Just forget it. I have to go." The stress of the situation was more than Willa could handle. She grabbed the twenty dollar bill and started to leave.

"Hang on just a minute there, honey," the clerk said. "I bet you were gonna go swimming today. It's hot out there. I was a teenager once." She smiled at Willa and reached into her purse under the checkout counter. She counted out the additional $1.19 from her own money. "Now give me that $20 and we'll call it even."

At this point, Willa was so overwhelmed she could barely speak. She handed the bill back to the cashier. "Thank you," she said and lowered her eyes to the conveyer belt in a mixture of deference and shame.

The empty belt rhythmically cycled around and around. It disappeared into the metal slot and returned again at the other end.

The cashier flipped a switch and the conveyor belt stopped moving. The noise from the cycling gears silenced.

"Don't you worry about it, hon." The cashier patted Willa's hand. "Someday you pay it forward to someone else, okay?"

Willa raised the sunglasses and placed them on top of her head. She had a sudden urge to cry. Why was this woman being so nice to her?

"Thank you again. You didn't have to do that," she said.

The cashier put the swimsuit in a bag and handed it to Willa. She looked into Willa's eyes now that the sunglasses no longer hid them. She paused with her hand in mid-air, the bag outstretched. "Say, wait a minute, do I know you?" she asked. She squinted and turned her head to the side.

"I don't think so," Willa said quickly. She grabbed the bag from the cashier and covered her eyes again with the sunglasses. Tucked the receipt in her pocket and began walking away.

"I do know you. Aren't you Debra Taylor's girl?" the cashier said. She was getting louder now as Willa hustled away. Willa still did not respond. She didn't even look back. Just kept walking, faster now, toward the door.

"Debra is worried sick about you, child. You need to call your momma!" The cashier was almost shouting now.

The automatic door swung open and Willa rushed into the parking lot. She jogged toward the car. Awkwardly in her flip flops. Unlocked the car and slid inside. She slammed the door shut and the world became quiet again. Her heart pounded in her chest. She gasped for air.

Willa sat in the car with her hands in her lap. Staring over the steering wheel, fighting to regain her composure.

A man pushed a row of shopping carts across the windshield. His arms outstretched, bent over, digging his heels to move the heavy row of carts. Willa watched him until he went inside the store.

She put the key in the ignition but did not start the engine. She took deep breaths, trying to calm herself. After a few seconds she reached into her front right pocket. She grabbed a half-empty Diet Coke from the drink holder in the center console. She took one gulp from the warm soda and swallowed hard. The little white pimple in her pocket was no more.

10

Cal knew his story would be more believable if he showed up to The Farm on foot. After turning on Natural Way, he pulled the MG off the road and parked behind a patch of trees. He had no trouble finding a spot to hide the car. The landscape in this part of the country was pure wilderness. The road was narrow—not even wide enough for two cars—and lined with trees on both sides. He piled a few branches on the vehicle to disguise it from the road.

Before walking the remaining half a mile to The Farm's entrance, Cal took one last look at the concealed MG and began the final leg of his journey.

As he walked, he thought about Penny's advice. How could he prove he had something to offer this group of recovering addicts? If they truly were as private and suspicious as Penny made them out to be, would he be able to pull off the disguise? If they saw through him, they might run him out of town like Penny had implied. Or they might do something even worse.

Cal already knew that word traveled fast in this small

town. The last thing he wanted was to endanger Willa. He wondered if she was at The Farm now. Maybe he would walk right in and find her.

He removed from his pocket the photograph Debra Taylor had given him. Willa's smiling face as she sat on the front steps of the Taylor home. Sandy blonde hair pinned with barrettes. Cut-off jean shorts and flip flops. Couldn't be more than sixteen in the photo. She certainly did not look like a drug addict. What if a few years of narcotics use had changed her appearance to the point Cal could no longer recognize her? He slid the photo back in his pocket and kept walking.

A hand-painted sign on a fence post marked the entrance to The Farm.

This Way to Healing

The dirt road led Cal through a break in the fence just wide enough for a pickup truck. The woods pressed in around him. The sounds of nature rose in the atmosphere as the woods thickened. The afternoon sun had begun to sink. Insects thrummed in the thick air, hearkening the approach of evening.

A few hundred yards down the dirt road, Cal encountered his first person: a woman crouched on her knees, bent over near the side of the road. She hunched forward, staring intently at the ground, moving her hands over the undergrowth before her.

Cal watched her as he approached. She stopped sweeping her hands across the ground long enough to palm some tiny object. She transferred the object to the folds of her dress and then continued searching the brush.

"Hello there," Cal called when he was within fifty feet of the woman.

She nearly jumped out of her skin. She fell backward on the ground. The bounty stowed in her dress scattered all around her. "My goodness, I didn't hear you walk up. You just about gave me a heart attack!" Her voice was shaky as she attempted to catch her breath, her body prostrate on the ground in front of Cal.

"Sorry about that. Didn't mean to startle you." Cal reached his arm out as he walked toward her. She took his hand and allowed him to help her up.

"Oh dear. My mushrooms. Will you help me gather them up?" She bent back down, plucking the fallen mushrooms and returning them to the pocket in the front of her cloth dress.

"Mushrooms, eh? I wondered what you were doing there." Cal knelt down beside the woman and helped her pick up the scattered fungi.

She squinted at him with a hint of suspicion in her eyes. "You were watching me? How long have you been here?"

Cal quickly raised his palms and responded. "Oh no, not at all. I was just walking up the road there and saw you working." He thumbed back over his shoulder in the direction he had come.

The woman still seemed suspicious. As she gathered up the last of the mushrooms she watched him out of the corner of her eye. When she finished, she stood up. She stretched her arms to relieve her back from the hunched position.

She looked to be in her early twenties. Her long, blonde hair hung down past her shoulders. Her cotton dress was worn thin, almost transparent in places. Sunlight filtered down through the tree canopy and lit her face. Her skin was tanned brown and a little dirty, like she had been working outside all day. No makeup or jewelry. Her dress hung loosely, and the piercing sunlight left no secret about the thin, feminine body underneath.

"Listen, I heard this is a place I can get some help," Cal said.

The woman's face instantly softened. The suspicion in her eyes faded and a smile spread across her face. "Yes. Yes, it is. You found us. You are among friends now." She opened her arms wide to give Cal a hug. "Welcome, brother."

This strange woman who a minute ago was ready to run Cal out of town now offered her arms in a hug. She smiled broadly, welcoming Cal. He accepted her outstretched arms and embraced her. She hugged him tightly, rubbing her hands across his back. He caught the faint smell of her natural body as they embraced. Not overpowering, just a slight, earthy human scent.

She took his hand. "This way, brother." She led him toward The Farm. "You are just in time for dinner. Are you hungry?"

Cal nodded.

Her hand gripped Cal's tightly. She pulled him down the road. She glanced back at him, still smiling, and asked, "Have you ever had fresh picked mushrooms?"

"I don't know. I don't think so."

"Oh boy, you are in for a treat," said the woman. "These are morels, and they are delicious. Nothing beats the taste of fresh food that you foraged for."

Cal didn't know what to say. He already felt a bit

overwhelmed by the whole situation.

The woman sensed his hesitancy. She said, "It's okay, friend. You will have a good night. You will sleep with a full belly and an easy mind tonight."

The dirt road rounded a bend and opened up to a lush, green field with a few sparse wooden buildings.

"Hey, everyone! We have a new brother here to join us tonight! He is hungry. We will feed him and welcome him!" the woman shouted to a group of people on the road ahead.

The group stood next to a dilapidated white barn with peeling paint and weathered wood. They raised their hands and waved to Cal and the woman.

She waved back. "Come on." She motioned for Cal to follow her and then broke into a jog toward the barn.

Cal approached the barn slowly.

Two men and three women including the one he had already met stood in a semicircle waiting to greet him. The men wore blue jeans and thin work shirts, and the women had on simple cloth dresses similar to the one worn by the first woman.

Cal fit right in with his worn jeans and flannel shirt. Good thing he had stopped at the thrift store on Penny's advice.

"This here is Eagle and High Life," the woman introduced Cal to the group. "And over there is Rabbit, Fawn, and Daisy."

Cal shook hands with the men and awkwardly hugged the women as they approached him in turn. "Nice to meet all of you. I'm going to need a good name like y'all have.

For now, we can just go with John."

"John," the woman known as Daisy repeated. "Don't worry, your new name will find you when you least expect it. Living here means shedding your old skin. Leaving your old life behind. And that includes the old name that keeps you rooted in the past."

The woman Cal had met on the road agreed. "That's right. Your new life begins now. Just wait till you meet Montana. He will explain everything." She looked up into Cal's eyes with her captivating gaze.

Her gaze drew Cal in and mesmerized him.

She took his hand again and led him past the barn. "Let's go to the house. We need to turn in the mushrooms we found so they can be used in the meal tonight."

The rest of the group had already proceeded a few steps ahead of them.

The woman pulled Cal along, keeping a tight grip on his hand. "You know, you didn't even ask my name," she said playfully as she walked.

"I guess I didn't."

Cal's mind reeled as he pondered his next step. He thought he would have more time to ease into this new disguise, but it was all happening fast.

"Well?" She stopped and looked back over her shoulder.

Cal smiled and played along. "What is your name?"

"Ren." She flashed her eyes at him again.

Cal resigned to Ren's pulling hand. He followed her toward the old farmhouse where he could see more people waiting for them to arrive.

*　*　*

A fire pit near the farmhouse crackled with burning logs. Smoke wafted above the pit and filled the air with its campfire smell.

As they approached the farmhouse Cal studied the activity taking place around them. Women and men—dressed similarly to those he had met—milled about, engaged in various pre-meal preparations. Dogs chased each other near the campfire, growling and playing with excitement at the coming meal.

Ready or not, Cal had been thrust right in the middle of the action. So much for easing into The Farm. It was now or never. He followed the group to the farmhouse.

Ren continued holding his hand, pulling him up to the covered front porch.

Some members of the group paused to observe him, the newcomer, as he approached.

"Listen up, y'all!" Ren announced as they walked. "We have a new visitor tonight. This is John. He is going to eat with us and hopefully stay awhile!"

The crew of people stopped working long enough to welcome Cal. A few shook hands or hugged him. Using that same hippie tone Ren used. Like they were exhaling the words rather than speaking them. Over the top with emotion and happiness.

"You any good at splitting wood?" asked one of the guys as he shook Cal's hand.

"I, uh, I think I can," Cal answered. He looked over at Ren hoping she would save him.

No luck there. Ren made no effort to extract Cal from the chore that awaited him.

"We all pitch in here. Share the load. It will help you work up an appetite," was all she said before she turned and ran up the stairs into the farmhouse.

Cal, left alone with the wood-chopping guy, shrugged his shoulders. He remembered Penny's advice to prove his value and show he could contribute to the group. "Have an extra axe?" he asked.

The guy smiled. Cal got the sense he had passed some kind of newcomer's test. He followed the guy around to the side of the house where two axes and a huge pile of firewood awaited them.

Cal had swung an axe before but he wasn't exactly a lumberjack. He watched the guy pick up his axe and take a piece of firewood from the pile.

The guy set the piece of wood on its flat end. Then he raised the axe high above his head. When he slammed the axe down on the piece of wood, he swung with such force that his feet briefly left the ground. The axe crashed into the wood, sending shrapnel flying in the air around them. When he finished the motion, his axe had sunk a few inches into the soft ground with a perfectly split log lying on either side of the axe head.

After watching a few swings, Cal grabbed the other axe and followed the guy's lead.

They chopped in silence for a couple of minutes. No sound other than the dull thud of the axes hitting the logs, and then the crack of splitting wood.

"I think we drew the short straw," Cal said after they had worked through about half the pile. "This is hard work."

The guy laughed but gave no response.

Cal straightened up and stretched his back. He stripped off the flannel, wiped the sweat from his face with it, and tossed the shirt on the ground next to his pile of split logs.

"You been out here long?" he asked the guy.

The guy stopped swinging his axe long enough to answer Cal's question. "A few months. I like it out here. Good people."

"I guess you stay in pretty good shape with this kind of work."

"Yep. It's good for me. My mind is too active. I need to keep myself busy or I get in trouble." The guy resumed swinging his axe.

"How many people live out here?" Cal asked.

The guy stopped again, looking a little perturbed this time. "Not sure. I don't really keep track of that. People come and go all the time. Every day. That is Montana's policy. Nobody stays longer than they want to. In order to get healed, you have to want it."

"Montana? Ren mentioned him too. He's in charge of this place?"

The guy rested his hands on the top of the axe handle. He looked at Cal with beads of sweat running down his face. The chest of his undershirt was damp and dirty. "You ain't from around here, are you?"

Cal started to get nervous. He had to be careful not to blow his cover. He again remembered Penny's words about how locals could tell an outsider from a mile away. "No, I'm not, to be honest with you," Cal answered. "I'm from a little further north. Drifted down this way looking for work. Got myself into a little trouble."

The guy watched Cal, quietly listening.

Cal continued, "I heard this was a place where a man could get help. So here I am."

The guy squinted his eyes slightly. He nodded. He seemed to be satisfied for now. He grabbed the axe and returned to his work. After a few swings, he spoke again. "That's alright, friend. You're alright now. Montana will want to meet you later. He'll be at dinner, and you can ask him all your questions then."

11

The late afternoon sun shone down on the little motel pool. Willa felt her skin tanning, soaking in the sun's heat. She liked the sensation. Almost too hot but it still felt good, like the sun was warming her body inside and out.

She wore her new swimsuit with the green polka dots. She lay on a vinyl deck chair—the kind with the straps that leave marks on your back when you roll over—with her sunglasses shielding her eyes. She had no plans to move a muscle unless she had to. She felt good. Nice and numb.

The pill had kicked in by the time she had returned to the motel. Luther was gone and she was glad. She had changed into the new suit immediately and headed for the pool, wanting to get down there before the drug sapped her motivation.

Willa kept her eyes open under the sunglasses watching the parking lot. No one else at the pool today, but she couldn't help noticing the creeps lurking around the motel.

Meth heads slammed doors as they went in and out. They stomped up and down the stairs. The same speed-freaks returned to the stash room time after time to get fixed.

"I need to get out of this shithole," Willa muttered to herself. "Bunch of creeps around here."

"What's that you said, honey?"

Willa sat up slightly. She turned her head to see a fat, hairy man leaning over the metal railing that surrounded the pool. The guy wore three gold chains around his neck. The chains glinted in the sunlight, almost lost in the tuft of black chest hair that overflowed from the top of his sleeveless white undershirt. Gold rings also adorned each of the man's fat fingers.

The guy stared at Willa with lecherous eyes that slowly roamed her body up and down. He moved his neck and head along with his eyes just to make it obvious how creepy he was.

"I said there's a bunch of creeps around here!" Willa repeated with disgust. She dropped back into the lounge chair and pretended to ignore the man.

"Maybe so. You just let me know if you need any help fighting 'em off." The man laughed and began coughing. Phlegm broke in his throat and he spat it out. Spit dribbled from his chin and stuck in his chest hair. He looked at Willa head-to-toe once more before sauntering off.

Willa was used to unwanted attention. Hanging around with Luther's crew she was often the only woman in the room, and most of Luther's friends were scum.

At least Eddie had treated her with respect, she thought, remembering her old boyfriend from the trailer park. Eddie didn't let anybody talk nasty to her. Her thoughts drifted back to Eddie and his trailer just on the other side of the park from her parents. She was so young when they met. Didn't have any idea what she was doing.

They did have some good times before she left him. Eddie wasn't much, but she could have made a life with him. She was pretty sure he loved her.

Now that was all gone. She had thrown it away. And she was stuck with this low-life Luther who didn't want to do anything but snort pills and fool around.

Willa unfastened the top of her swimsuit. She lifted the strap to see if she was getting sunburned. The strip of skin beneath the strap was pale. Just a little longer, she thought. She closed her eyes. Felt the hot sun on her body. Her skin was cooking but it felt good. Like being in a sauna. Dry heat warming her all the way to the bones.

Eddie crept into her mind again. Why was she thinking about him so much? Probably her brain looking for a way out of this screwed up life she had gotten herself into. It wasn't even that long ago she was at Eddie's trailer. A month, not even that. Maybe she could go back. Her parents were there, too. Willa knew her parents worried about her. She didn't need the Walmart cashier to remind her of that.

The last time she tried to leave Luther had found her. He came and got her at the hippie commune out in the country. The place was full of weirdos but they were straight at least. And they were going to help her. But Luther had found her within a day. So much for getting off pills. Luther handed her one the second she got in his car. Twenty-four hours of sobriety down the drain.

"Baby doll, you're gonna be a lobster. I can see that pink skin from here," Luther hollered over to her, breaking her daydream. He got out of the car and slammed the door. He held a plastic bag at his side with a yellow smiley face on it.

Speak of the devil, Willa thought. She sat up and had to catch her top to keep it from falling off without the straps fastened. "It's called a suntan. You should try it sometime. You look like a pasty white marshmallow."

"Uh oh, she got her a new swimsuit and now she's feeling feisty."

Luther carried the bag toward the metal stairs, swinging it dramatically at his side.

"Quit hollering so the whole place hears you," Willa shouted back. "What's in the bag anyway since you're so damn proud of it?"

"You wouldn't like it."

"Get your skinny little butt over here and don't tell me what I like."

Luther cracked a sly smile, proud that he had gotten Willa's attention. He walked over to the pool and leaned on the black fence where the fat, hairy guy had been a few minutes before. He reached his hand in the bag and slowly pulled down the plastic to reveal a six-pack of Miller Lite tallboys. He lifted the sixer and presented it before him like a magician pulling a rabbit out of a hat. "Ta-Da," he said.

"Give me one of those," Willa reached out her hand.

"You're awfully grabby, ain't you?"

"It's hot out here. I'm thirrrsty." Willa dragged out the word with a slight pout.

"I bet you are. Here." Luther tore a beer off the plastic ring and handed it over the fence. "I'm going up. Don't be too long. I got some guys coming over to see us tonight. We need to get ready."

Willa took the beer. She popped the top and swallowed a long drink from the ice cold can. "What guys?" she asked.

"Don't worry about it. Just don't get all sunburned so

you look like a fool."

Willa frowned. She took another sip of beer. "Whatever."

She leaned back in her chair and kicked her legs up on the vinyl straps. She rested the beer on her protruding hip bone.

The sun was sinking. It was stealing away the last of her poolside afternoon. She sipped the beer and watched the fluorescent lights flicker on at the gas station across the street.

12

At The Farm, dinner was served outside on a hand-built wooden table around back of the farmhouse. Huge, split logs formed the tabletop. They were sanded to a silky soft surface, then sealed and stained with a clear coat of lacquer that felt as smooth as ice and shined bright enough to hold a reflection. At over thirty feet long, the table seated a party's worth of people on the benches lining either side of it.

By the time Cal and his wood-chopping buddy rounded the back of the house, most of the table was already full of people. Cal saw serving dishes piled high with vegetables and potatoes. The smell of roasted herbs filled the air. Cal had worked up an appetite. He was ready to eat.

Cal followed his partner over to an outdoor water pump where the two took turns pumping water to clean up. The water took a few seconds to rise up the rusted pipe from deep within the earth. After five or six pumps of the iron handle liquid burst forth from the red spigot. Ice cold and pure.

The water felt great as Cal splashed it on his face and neck. He used the flannel to dry off, and then he put the shirt back on. The cool dampness soothed his aching shoulders and back. His arms felt like dead weight at his sides after swinging the axe for an hour. He couldn't imagine doing it every day.

Turning toward the dinner party, Cal spotted Ren seated near the head of the table. She waved at him and patted the empty spot next to her on the bench. He walked over and eased himself on to the seat. One foot over the bench and then the other. He could feel his hamstrings tightening from the workout.

"How do you feel?" asked Ren, smiling.

"Like I just chopped enough firewood to last a year." Cal exhaled a tired sigh.

"Don't worry, that will only last us for tonight. There will be plenty more to chop tomorrow." Ren winked and patted Cal's thigh under the table.

Just then, all chatter at the table ceased. Even the dogs stopped chasing each other and sat quietly. Cal looked up, acutely aware of the sudden silence.

"He's here," Ren whispered.

Cal followed Ren's eyes up the stairs to the back porch of the farmhouse. Standing at the top of the stairs was a man with long, blonde hair. He wore a colorful Mexican-style poncho and a pair of well-worn blue jeans. No shoes. He had a bushy beard and his skin was tanned a golden brown.

The man raised his hands to the group. Both hands over his head, palms out. "Welcome, all. Thank you for being here. Thank you for this delicious feast, and for the brothers and sisters with whom we share it." He lowered his hands slowly and then stepped down the stairs. He moved with a calculated grace, as though he felt the eyes of everyone upon him.

When he reached the bottom of the stairs, the table filled with talking and laughter, but with a renewed excitement and energy. The man, who Cal figured had to be Montana, sat at the head of the table just two seats away from Cal.

Cal watched him cautiously. He caught a waft of patchouli from Montana's poncho.

As soon as Montana took his seat, the feast began.

Cal had never seen so much food on a table. Platters piled high with meats and vegetables like some Viking warrior bounty.

Cal stabbed a chunk of meat with his fork and dragged it to his plate. "This is quite a feast you have here. Is this normal?" he asked the table nonchalantly.

"Nature provides, my friend," said Montana to Cal's left.

The rest of the table became quiet when Montana spoke.

"You must be in pretty good with Mother Nature, eh?" Cal asked Montana directly this time.

Montana smiled patronizingly. He closed his eyes, still smiling, and nodded slowly without speaking.

Ren pulled at Cal's right elbow. "Don't forget the mushroom gravy for your meat. These are the mushrooms we picked today." She quickly began spooning gravy over the meat on Cal's plate.

She was trying to distract Cal from his exchange with Montana. As a newcomer, maybe he wasn't supposed to address the man directly.

Cal allowed the interruption and followed Ren's lead. He turned his attention to the food in front of him. He didn't want to rock the boat just yet.

But Montana wasn't finished with him. "I see we have a new face at the table today. Welcome, brother." He spoke slowly, deliberately, emphasizing each word. "Tell us your name and how you found your way to The Farm."

Montana addressed Cal but he looked around the table as he spoke. He made eye contact with each person one at a time before slowly moving on to the next. He behaved like a keynote speaker working his audience. His gaze finally rested on Cal. He stared into Cal's eyes waiting for him to answer.

"Well, uh, my name is John. I spent some time working in factories up north in Ohio. Youngstown mainly. Union jobs are hard to find nowadays. I drifted around for a while. It's tough out there. Headed further south for warmer weather. Been doing some tobacco picking around here lately. Talk about grueling labor. The pay is peanuts. Mostly migrant labor. No way I can compete with migrant workers when it comes to pay scale."

The table was quiet, listening to the conversation between Cal and their leader.

Cal continued, "Eventually I landed here hoping to find work in the coal mines. So far, I have only managed to get myself deeper in trouble."

The table nodded in agreement. They murmured words of encouragement and solidarity. Cal realized his story hit home for many of The Farm's inhabitants. He guessed a lot of them had similar experiences, especially here in the coal country of Eastern Kentucky. When the work dries up, people get desperate. And when people get desperate, they are ripe for exploitation.

Montana nodded once, his piercing eyes still fixed on Cal. "You found us. You are safe now. The meal you see before you, this is yours every day when you dine with brothers and sisters at The Farm." He swept his hand over the table majestically. "In exchange, all we ask for is your loyalty, your sobriety, and your participation in our household chores. We share the load, and we share the bounty."

Cal nodded. "Seems like a fair deal to me. Thank you."

Cal was appreciative of the food if a little annoyed by Montana's superior tone and the godlike reverence paid to him by his followers. But he was here for a short time only. Just long enough to ask around about Willa. He didn't need to make long-lasting friendships. He only had to keep his mouth shut and play the game for a day or so.

"You are welcome to stay as long as you can. Our way of life is not for everyone," said Montana.

Cal got the impression Montana was poking at him, pushing him to see if Cal was for real. The man had been staring at him throughout the entire conversation. His intensity began to feel a little creepy.

"I already got a chance to participate in the household chores. Swinging an axe is no joke. Maybe tomorrow I can wash dishes instead?" Cal tried to lighten the mood. He got a laugh from the table, but Montana merely smiled his patronizing smile.

After the laughter subsided, Montana spoke again. "Maybe so, Badger. Maybe so."

Cal glanced around apprehensively, wondering if he had heard Montana correctly. "Badger?" he asked.

"The land has spoken to me. Your new name has been

granted. Badger will be your name as long as you stay with us."

Cal had no response. How could he? He nodded quietly and began eating his dinner. If this Montana fellow wanted to mess with him, Cal just needed to suck it up. Stick to the plan. Eat the meal, ask around about Willa Taylor, and then get out of there as soon as he could. After all, he was eating their food for free and everyone else seemed decent so far. It could be worse.

Ren leaned over and whispered with excitement into Cal's ear, "It's rare to get a name this soon. Mother Earth has blessed you." She smiled broadly and kissed Cal on the cheek.

No one at the table seemed to notice. This kind of exchange appeared to be common at The Farm. This young woman, whom Cal had only met a few hours prior, was getting friendly fast. A little weird for sure, but Cal could think of a lot worse places to be right now.

Cal turned toward Ren. Her eyes were radiant, slightly mischievous. He returned her smile.

Ren scooted over so her hips touched Cal's. She patted his thigh again under the table, and this time left her hand resting on his tight quadricep. She rubbed her fingers softly, methodically over his faded blue jeans.

The sun set on the horizon as they ate, cascading vibrant hues of red, pink, and orange over the field.

Chatter and laughter filled the table. With the hard day's work in the books, it was now time for relaxation and fellowship.

Cal listened to the conversations around him, carefully eavesdropping for any references to Willa or to a girl who might fit her description. He stuffed himself with the delicious feast, feeling good and mellow. His only wish would be to wash the feast down with a bottle of red wine, knowing full well that was an impossible daydream at this drug-free commune.

Throughout the meal Ren's hand crept slowly up Cal's thigh.

After dinner, the group moved over to the fire pit. The conversations got quieter as the night darkened. People broke off into smaller groups and stretched out in front of the fire to wind down the evening. Children scurried about, laughing and playing in the background just outside the glow of the fire.

Cal stared into the raging bonfire. He allowed his mind to wander. With a blaze like that it's no wonder they chop so much firewood around here, he thought.

Ren approached Cal from behind, sliding her arms around his waist. She pressed her head against his shoulder blades. "See what you did for us?" she said. She lifted her right hand off Cal's midsection and pointed toward the fire. "You gave us fire tonight. All the pleasure you see around us, you helped create it." She spoke into Cal's shoulder as she pointed, then returned her hand to his stomach and squeezed.

"That might be taking it a bit far," Cal said. He gripped Ren's hands, pulling them tighter around him. He had to admit he liked the way this hippie girl thought. It felt good to make something with his hands that others could appreciate.

"Just wait. You'll see. You will get used to this way of life. We make everything from scratch and we help each other. We bring pleasure to each other's lives."

"I can probably get used to that idea," Cal whispered over his shoulder.

Ren laughed and pulled away from him. She took Cal's hand and led him up to the fire where a group of people were seated.

"Hey, y'all. Mind if we join you?" Ren asked as they approached the group.

"Not at all. Grab a seat."

There was only one open chair. Cal offered it to Ren. She shook her head and sat him down in it, then settled into his lap.

"Badger, you play any instruments?" asked a guy nearby. He was tuning a guitar on his lap. He looked up at Cal as he spoke.

"Not really."

"No music at all?" asked another woman in the group.

"I mean, well, I like music. Does that help?"

"Good enough!" shouted the first guy. "Somebody give him the djembe."

They passed a round drum with a wooden base over to Cal and Ren. Ren took it and gripped it between her thighs where she held it firmly.

"Look, like this," she said. She opened her palm and tapped the tight skin on the drumhead. It resonated deeply with a thunk.

"Ok, but I'm not making any promises," Cal said. He repeated Ren's example and thumped the djembe. The sound was warm and full.

"Alright, man, you got it!" said the first guy. "Now just follow along."

The man began strumming the guitar. Another guy

played mandolin. It was a folksy bluegrass song with a dark, haunting undertone. Both men sang and a woman began to harmonize with them. They sang about a union strike in the coal mines, asking which side are you on, telling the listener he must choose to either stand with the strikers or else fight against them.

Cal did his best to keep a rhythm on the drum. He played it quietly, knowing he was outmatched by his musical counterparts. Ren rested her head on his chest and hummed softly along with the music. Her hair had a fresh and slightly citrus scent like tea tree oil.

When the song ended, another one immediately began. Cal wondered, who are these people that they all have amazing voices and musical talent? He quietly set the djembe off to the side. He had made an effort at least. Ren felt good in his lap. Her face pressed against his chest, the warm fire crackled in front of him. The soft voices gently serenaded them. It was easy to relax here, that's for sure.

But Cal couldn't let himself get too comfortable. He was here for a reason. He needed to start talking to The Farm's residents. Time to ask some questions about Willa. He put his hand on Ren's shoulder and sat up slowly in the chair.

She shifted with his movements, continuing to rest against his body.

Cal leaned to his right, away from the music, and got the attention of a nearby couple. "Sure is a nice night, eh?" he said.

The man and woman smiled and nodded in agreement. The fire danced across their faces.

"How long have you all been living out here?" Cal asked.

"Oh, a few months now I guess," said the man. "We actually met each other here." He took the woman's hand. "I'm not sure I would have made it without her help. I was in pretty bad shape when I got here."

"Yeah?" Cal pushed for more information.

"The drugs had a hold of me."

"Pills?"

The man nodded.

"You kicked the habit?" Cal asked.

"I take things one day at a time, friend. But I haven't used in three months."

"Good for you," Cal answered, genuinely happy for the man. This place seemed to have a way of helping people.

After a few seconds, Cal spoke again. "Do you see a lot of people coming through here?"

The man nodded. "Yes, it's not for everyone."

"People keep saying that. What do you mean by it exactly?"

"It means that not everyone can handle this way of life. We don't have a shopping mall or computers or video games. Some people just can't take it."

"And no drugs allowed," said the woman.

"That, too." said the man. "People think because this is like a hippie commune that it's okay to smoke a little grass or whatever you want. But Montana will throw your butt right out if he catches you. There is no place for drugs of any kind here."

"I see. No argument here," Cal said.

"Good. If you are willing to play by the rules, you can be happy here," said the woman.

"How will I know if I break the rules?" Cal asked.

"You'll know."

Cal was silent for a few minutes. He stroked Ren's shoulder and stared into the fire. It crackled and popped loudly. Smoke wafted up into the air around them.

He turned back to the couple. "I met a woman who passed through here recently. I wonder if you remember her?" he asked. "Pretty, thin, blonde about nineteen years old. Likes the pills."

"You just described most of the women here, bud," answered the man.

"Her name is Willa. Does that sound familiar at all?" Cal continued.

The man quickly turned his head away from Cal and faced the fire. He gave no answer.

"Do you remember her?" Cal prodded.

The man looked over at the woman next to him. They exchanged a nervous glance. She sighed and spoke, "Yes, we know that girl."

"You do? Was she here?"

"She was. Until about a week ago."

"What happened?" Cal sat up in his chair.

"She couldn't follow the rules," was the only response given.

"Listen, I really need to find her. Do you know what happened to her?"

"Hey man, cool out. We don't keep track of everyone around here. People come and go."

"But you know her. You said she couldn't follow the rules. Did something happen to her?" Cal was getting agitated.

Ren sensed his agitation and sat up. "Baby, what's going on? No need to get upset," she soothed.

Cal was in danger of blowing his cover. He needed to

regain control of the situation. "No worries, just a friend of mine I was curious what happened to her." He turned back to the couple. "Sorry about that. She's a fellow traveler and I lost her on the road."

"You'll find her again if it's meant to be," Ren said. She took Cal's face in both hands and straightened his head so he was looking directly into her eyes.

Cal's body relaxed as he stared into Ren's eyes. He sunk into the chair. The music flooded back in and enveloped him in its warm rhythm.

Ren leaned forward. She nuzzled her nose gently against Cal's cheek.

Cal turned his face to the side and met her lips with his. They kissed. He opened his eyes to see her smiling softly at him.

Ren whispered in his ear, "I have a spot for us saved in the barn's loft."

She took Cal's hand and pulled him up out of the chair.

Cal and Ren headed away from the fire toward the barn. They climbed the ladder and fell into each other's arms on a pile of soft hay.

Above their heads, the starry sky peeked in through cracks in the old boards, dimly lighting the loft. The stars watched over the couple as they held each other tightly in a passionate embrace.

13

Willa hung her bathing suit on the towel rack and turned on the shower. She stood in the bathroom with the door closed, allowing the steam to fill the tiny space.

She sipped another of the Miller Lite tallboys that Luther had brought home. Her second one of the day. She set the beer on the sink and sat down on the closed toilet lid. She stared at the floor, inhaling the steam, letting it calm her nerves and soothe her body.

She thought about Eddie again. And then about her parents. Poor Elroy and Debra. They had no idea where Willa was. She had just run off. Taken what was left from the pill bottle in her dad's medicine cabinet and vanished. She had been sneaking the pills one by one carefully up until that point. Paying attention to the way items were arranged in the cabinet, making sure to replace them exactly as she had found them.

Willa was only eleven years old when her dad got hurt at the mines. She didn't understand what had happened. How could she? All she knew was the big, strong man she had known for a decade was now lying in bed and couldn't even get up to use the bathroom. She watched her mom's life change as Debra took care of Elroy after the injury. Her dad became totally dependent on Debra while he went through rehab to get back on his feet.

It wasn't until age sixteen that she learned about all the medications her dad took for the pain. Smoking pot one time with Eddie, he asked her point blank what all meds her dad was on. Why did he care, she wanted to know. Eddie said he knew a guy who would buy those pain pills for top dollar if she could sneak some out. One pill could make them $100, a whole bottle could be their ticket to Lexington. Get them out of the trailer park where they could start a new life. Eddie knew that was Willa's goal, to go to college at the University of Kentucky.

It took a few more times of Eddie asking before she finally swiped one of her dad's pills. Terrified the whole time. Her dad at work and her mom at the grocery. She went in the bathroom, found the pill bottle, unscrewed the cap and lifted one of the tiny pills.

She took it straight to Eddie. An hour later, they had a $100 dollar bill lying on the kitchen table in Eddie's trailer. It was the first time Willa had ever seen one. Benjamin Franklin with his bald head, smiling up at her from the green paper. A few weeks later, she stole another pill. And not long after that another, and another. The bottle in the medicine cabinet just kept refilling, so she wasn't worried about it. Not like she was depriving her dad of anything. He had an endless supply. Why not turn them into a little cash, prime the pump on her college fund.

The first time she swallowed one of the pills a whole new world opened up to her. The floating euphoria she felt was unlike anything she had ever experienced. All worries and all pain, gone. She felt happy. She could talk to anyone about anything, go anywhere and do anything. It was the best feeling she had ever known. She understood exactly why the pills were so valuable. She could never afford the price tag on her own. Lucky for her she had a bottomless supply for free.

Eddie was furious when he found out Willa had swallowed one. Willa knew she shouldn't have told Eddie about it. He had already made it clear what he thought about the scum who bought their pills. Eddie hated the pillheads. He hated their weakness, the way they threw everything away for the drug, paid any amount of money.

But Willa wasn't one of those addicts. Just one pill. And it felt great. She only told him because she wanted him to feel the euphoria she felt. The sensation was too good to keep to herself. She wanted to share it with him.

"But Eddie," she had said, "it feels sooo good. Like there's nothing in the world can hurt you."

He told her to get out of his trailer and don't come back if she ever swallowed another pill. He told her about the heads he saw when he went to unload the stolen pills, how strung out they are, how they can't even stand up. Shuffling along, falling down, slurring words, how they would do anything for their next fix. Is that what you want to happen to you, he asked her.

"Geez, Eddie, it's just one pill. For god's sake, calm down," she said with that slow, euphoric tone in her voice. The voice that says I feel no pain.

"That's how it starts," he said. "I'm telling you, Willa, do not fuck around with these things. Once you start rolling that rock down the hill it picks up speed fast."

"Alright, already! Take a—" she almost said chill pill but

changed her mind, "take a cold shower and relax. I won't eat another one."

That was two years ago. It turned out she was wrong about being able to quit.

And Eddie was right.

Pounding on the bathroom door snapped Willa out of the daydream.

"What the hell's going on in there? Don't use all the hot water!" shouted Luther on the other side of the thin wooden door.

Willa sat up on the toilet seat. She took a long swig from the beer. The alcohol kicked the pain pill's effects into high gear. Her body started to float. She felt warm and numb.

"I said don't use all the hot water!" Luther shouted again.

"What do you care. It's not like you ever take a shower," Willa said, not loud enough for Luther to hear. Then, louder, "Almost done."

She pulled back the shower curtain and stepped into the steaming hot water. She turned her face up to the shower head and let the water wash over her. Down her shoulders, chest, hips, and legs. Swirling, swirling into the bathtub and down the drain.

When Willa opened the bathroom door, the trapped steam rushed out around her. She stepped off the moist tile and onto the filthy brown carpet of the motel room with a towel wrapped around her body and another on her hair.

Beads of water dotted her bare shoulders and the top of her chest. It streamed down her legs and dripped on the carpet with each step.

By the time she heard the voices it was already too late to retreat. She turned to face the sounds, wearing only the two towels.

Three strangers lounged in the room talking to Luther. He was leaned against the dresser at the foot of the bed, facing the group of men. Willa didn't recognize any of them.

Two guys sat at the small kitchenette table. The other one was stretched out on the bed, fully clothed with his boots on. His slick, snakeskin boots were kicked up on the bedspread with his legs crossed at the ankles. He was leaned back against the headboard with his hands laced behind his head. He smiled broadly at Willa, knowing she had been caught off guard, enjoying her surprised reaction.

"And what do we have here?" the guy on the bed said with a heavy Southern drawl. He looked Willa up and down and whistled.

Willa glanced down at the carpet nervously, then up at Luther. "Why didn't you tell me we had company?"

The guy on the bed answered for Luther. "Cause he wanted to do us a favor, and I, for one, am right glad he did."

"How about you put your eyes back in their sockets before I teach you some manners," Willa snapped.

The guys at the table broke out in laughter. "Better watch out, Merle," one shouted as he pounded the table.

Merle shot them a look that silenced their laughter. He turned to Luther, "You got you a live one, don't ya?"

"She's got a mouth on her, alright," said Luther.

Willa grabbed her jeans, a top, and some underwear from the dresser and went back in the bathroom. She could hear the guys out in the room talking and laughing while she dressed.

"That's the beauty of it," one of the guys at the table was saying when Willa re-opened the bathroom door. "You got them coming and going. Two jobs at the same time."

"Plus all the customers," said the guy on the bed who had been identified as Merle. "They all got wallets and purses and jewelry."

The group of men stopped talking and acknowledged Willa again as she came back in the room.

"Shame you had to go and put on all those clothes," said Merle. "I kind of liked you more the first time."

"Hey, knock it off, alright?" said Luther.

Merle held up his hands and grinned. "Just saying, man. You got you a lovely lady. Don't mind me." His tone did not sound apologetic. He kept his eyes on Willa. Licked his lips slightly as he watched her.

This time Willa was ready for him. She stared right back at him and said, "What kind of name is Merle anyway?" She put her hands on the sink behind her and raised herself up to sit on the countertop. The mirror reflected her shoulders and the back of her head to the room.

"It's the name given to my father, and then he gave it to me. You got a problem with it?" said Merle. He narrowed his eyes as he challenged her. "Anyway, you never heard of Merle Haggard?"

"Yeah, I have," said Willa. "But it sounds dumber on you. It doesn't fit you. I guarantee you ain't no Merle

Haggard."

"Shew, you're a big talker for such a little girl," said Merle.

Luther looked over at Willa and told her to be quiet. Then he turned back to the guys at the table. "You're telling me you want to hit the bowling alley on Saturday night when it's full of people?"

"Yeah buddy. Between the bar, the cashier, and all the customers, there's at least ten grand in there on a busy night. Maybe more."

"But what about all the people? How in the hell are you going to run traffic control on a crowd that size?"

Merle answered with a question of his own. "When was the last time you went bowling?"

"Every Tuesday with the church league," said Luther with sarcasm. "I don't know, man, what difference does it make?"

"It makes a difference cause on Saturday night, they do the laser light shit," said Merle. "They turn off all the lights and crank up the music so fuckin' loud you can't even hear a strike in the next lane. Between the laser lights and disco balls spinning around, nobody in that place has any idea what's happening around them."

"Easy money," said one of the table guys.

"How's it work then?" said Luther.

"Well, my friend, I'm glad you asked," said Merle. "The way I figure we've got three operations running at the same time. The front desk, the bar, and the lanes. So we need three teams. You know, we want to get in and get out. So we get all three teams working at the same time rather than moving one to the next. In and out."

Merle paused and looked around the room to see if

everyone was following him. Willa slid off the counter and grabbed another beer from the ring of Miller Lites. She returned to her perch and popped the beer loudly.

"You got everything you need over there, little miss?" said Merle.

"Yup, thanks for asking," said Willa.

"Just want to make sure you're all situated and happy," said Merle. He winked at her and she rolled her eyes.

Luther got them back on track, saying, "Three teams, fine, but there are four of us. How do we divide up?"

"I'll get to that," said Merle. First, though, I like the way your lady thinks. Let's all have us a beverage, eh? Freshen up our drinks a little."

He removed a flask from his back pocket, uncapped it, and took a long swig. Raising the flask in Willa's direction, he swallowed hard and exhaled forcefully to punctuate the burn of the alcohol. Twisting the cap back on the flask, he said, "What's your name anyway, Doll?"

"Willa."

"Well, Willa. Here's to you. You already met me— Merle, just like the great Merle Haggard. This here is Randy and Jandy." Merle nodded toward the two guys at the table as he spoke. "Randy's the brains, and Jandy's the braun."

The two goons raised their hands and waved in turn as they were introduced. They could have been twins. Big cornbread-eating rednecks. Fat guys with beards who looked like they had never left the county since the day they were born.

Willa watched quietly and sipped the beer.

"Okay, now where was I?" said Merle.

"Three teams," said Randy.

"Right. So we've got three teams. Now, the front desk

clerk, that's just some teenager with pimples. Lives in his parents' basement and plays dungeons and dragons or some shit like that. Never been in a real tussle in his life. He sits there and sprays an aerosol can into sweaty shoes all night. This guy ain't a threat. Walk up to him, put a gun in his face, and he's handing you the cash before you can tell him your shoe size. The front desk team only requires one guy."

Merle took another swig from the flask. He looked round the room for effect, trying to build some excitement before continuing.

When he was sure everyone was listening, he said, "The bar, on the other hand, is gonna be full of people. There's no way we can pull that job without being noticed. So we put two guys in the bar. One to work the bartender, and the other to manage the crowd."

"One guy takes the cash and the other robs the drinkers," said Luther. "Watches and wallets, that kind of thing?"

"Now you're catching on, my friend," said Merle. "That's a total of three people so far. Brings us to the final team: team three. That'll take two more guys. They start on opposite ends of the lanes. Twenty-four lanes in the place, so that's twelve each and they meet in the middle. This is the most time-consuming job of the three. Lots of touches, lots of interactions. They each take a bag and just run right down the line."

Merle stopped talking. He waited for questions.

"How long will it take?" asked Luther.

"Ten minutes tops. Three teams, all running at the same time. Meet at the front door and get out before anyone has a chance to do anything. Remember, the laser lights are shining and the music is blaring the whole time. Nobody even sees it coming until they're already hit."

"What do you think?" said Randy to Luther.

Willa cut in and spoke first. "I think you assholes are gonna blow it and end up dead or in jail."

The room was silent for a few moments. Everyone waiting for Merle to respond, wondering how he would react to Willa's interruption.

"Us assholes, huh?" said Merle finally. "One, two, three," he was pointing at each person in the room as he counted. When he got to Willa, he stopped, pointing directly at her, "Five. Three teams, five people."

"Hell no," said Willa. "You think I'm going to be part of this crazy scheme? You are out of your mind."

"Now, see, that's what I thought you might say," said Merle. "But Luther here, he seems to think you might change your mind. He says he has something you need. Something you might be willing to do anything to get back if it were to be taken away from you."

Willa felt a chill run through her body at the thought of her pill supply being cut off. That had to be what this creep Merle was talking about. The fear began to take hold of her. Skipping a day or two would make her body start hurting bad. The withdrawal from pain pills was brutal. Like all the pain you had avoided while on them was saving up, and it hit you all at once when you came off them.

Willa sipped her beer quietly. She was reluctant to get involved. It was the last thing she wanted to do. But if it was the only way to keep getting drugs…

After a few moments, she spoke again. Staring down at the floor, almost mumbling, "Don't you have some other henchman to use? I don't even know how to fire a gun. I wouldn't be much help."

"On the contrary, I think you will be a valuable asset. Might even say you are perfect for the job," said Merle. "You and Luther work the bar. He can get the cash and you handle the crowd. They'll be checking you out the whole time, wondering what this sexy little lady is doing robbing a bowling alley. You won't even have to use the gun. Just hold it for a little while and make yourself two grand."

Two thousand dollars for ten minutes work. Willa had to admit that sounded pretty good. But these guys? They were walking time bombs. No chance they could pull off a complicated job like this without getting caught. "I think I'll pass," she said.

"We'll see about that," said Merle. "It's Thursday now so we've got a little under forty-eight hours. Think about it." He looked at Luther and nodded.

Willa tried to get Luther's attention, but he wouldn't turn her way. He stayed focused on Merle.

"That's it for now. Don't go telling anybody what we talked about, you hear?" Merle said to Willa. "I'll see you Saturday."

Willa made a face at him when he turned his back to stand up from the bed.

"Come on, boys, let's go get into some trouble," Merle said to Randy and Jandy.

The three men stood and left the motel room without another word. The door slammed behind them, leaving Luther and Willa alone again.

"Surely you aren't dumb enough to go along with those guys," said Willa after a few seconds. "You really think they can pull off a job that big without screwing it up?"

Luther shrugged. "Four thousand bucks for us,

though."

"Only if you get out of there alive. You don't know what the hell you're doing robbing a place. Have you ever even pointed a gun at somebody?"

"How hard can it be? You heard him. All the lights and music. We're in and out in ten minutes."

"First of all there is no 'we'. I told you I'm not getting involved with this half-brained scheme. Especially not with those three clowns as partners," said Willa. She was feeling drunk from the beer now, getting confident and letting her true feelings come out.

"But we need a fifth man. And that's why this works, cause you and me are together but we each get a fifth of the jack. That's forty percent of the payoff to us," said Luther.

"Hey, he can actually do math," said Willa. She hopped off the counter and approached Luther, still carrying the beer in her left hand. With her right hand, she poked Luther in the ribs as she passed him. He swatted her hand away and watched silently as she walked over to the window. When she got to the window, she pulled the curtain aside to look out.

It was dark outside. Willa could see the moon reflecting in the swimming pool below. Yellow street lights cast shadows in the parking lot. Merle and his minions were nowhere in sight. She let the curtain drop and turned back to Luther. "And second of all, how do you even know this Merle dude? Who's to say he isn't planning on making us take the fall? Or what if he just grabs the money and runs?"

"Merle has done robberies before. He knows how to make them work. Like he said, it takes three teams. It won't work unless everybody does their part."

"Are you listening to yourself? You are as dumb as they are."

Willa finished off the beer and set it down on the table with a metallic clink. She stood with her hand on her hip, staring at Luther. Challenging him.

Anger flashed in Luther's eyes. He jumped up and stormed across the motel room toward Willa. She saw him coming and quickly retreated, cowering behind the chair to avoid him.

"I'm sorry! I didn't mean it!" she yelled as he approached.

Luther grabbed the chair with one hand and flung it aside. It tumbled over and slammed into the dresser with a loud crash. He pinned Willa against the wall next to the window. His face was inches from hers. He breathed rapidly, seething with rage.

"I've had about enough of you tonight," he growled. His breath smelled sour and hot. Willa turned her head to avoid it.

"You think you can talk like that in front of my friends? Embarrass me that way?" Luther's grip tightened on Willa's throat.

"No, I'm sorry. I'm sorry. I had too many beers. I shouldn't have," Willa cried hoarsely, her windpipe closing. She choked out the words.

"Goddamn right," said Luther. He released his grip and Willa crumpled to the floor at his feet, gasping for air.

"Now don't make me do that to you again," said Luther. He stood above her, staring down, eyes bulging, chest heaving from adrenaline. "I'm doing this job on Saturday and so are you. We'll get our four grand and buy a shitload of drugs with it. No more questions and no more backtalk."

Luther snatched the TV remote off of the dresser and sat down on the bed where Merle had been a few minutes before. He leaned over the nightstand and examined the glass surface, carefully scanning for drug residue. He dragged his finger around the glass, scooping remnants of white powder into a line. He rolled up a dollar bill and snorted the rail.

Luther leaned his head back, letting the powder slide through his sinuses and down the back of his throat. He kicked his feet up on the bedspread. Put a pillow behind his back to prop up his neck. He turned on the television and flipped channels until he landed on an old black and white western film. He stared at the screen, not speaking, not even acknowledging Willa's presence in the room.

Willa laid on the floor where she had fallen. She didn't dare provoke Luther again tonight. She knew once he snapped like that, it was better to stay far away from him.

The dirty carpet smelled like cigarettes and vomit. She could see hairballs, crumbs, and ash twisted into the brown fibers. Willa put her arm under her head and curled into a ball. She closed her eyes and tried to shut out the world around her. The air conditioner hummed by her head. The cool air felt good blowing on her sun-tanned shoulders.

After an hour or so of lying there in petrified silence, Willa dozed off to the sound of the television: Hollywood six-shooters and the bugle call of the cavalry that never seemed to arrive.

14

Cal opened his eyes to sunlight streaming in through cracks in the barn's wooden roof. First light at The Farm, and the day's activity had already begun. Cal heard signs of life in the field below him. Roosters crowing and people talking with the hushed voices of early morning.

He sat up and surveyed his surroundings. A colorful Native American blanket covered him to the chest. Another blanket lay beneath him, spread atop a billowed pile of hay. The hay felt soft and had a dry, sweet smell. It crackled as he moved.

Cal was alone in the loft. Ren's side of the blanket lay open where she had slipped out, the blanket still warm from her body heat.

Cal reached for his flannel shirt and pulled it on to ward off the slight morning chill. His shirt held the campfire scent of the previous night. He peeled back the blanket and stood up in the loft wearing only the flannel and his underwear.

He stretched and stepped into his hiking boots. Leaving the laces undone, he shuffled over to the open window in the barn's loft and looked out.

Below him, people milled about rebuilding the fire, gathering eggs from the henhouse, sipping coffee out of tin mugs. Cal fumbled with the buttons on his flannel as he surveyed the field—his first real chance to look around without someone watching his every move.

Cal spotted Ren standing in the doorway of the farmhouse. She faced inside the building. The sunlight shone through her dress, revealing the outlines of her smooth, brown legs. She wore a gray cardigan over top of the dress. It hung loosely at her sides, unbuttoned. The sleeves were too long for her arms. They swallowed her hands and exposed only the tips of her cupped fingers below the open cuffs. Ren was speaking to someone in the house, but Cal couldn't see who.

He watched for a few seconds, wondering who Ren was chatting with already this morning. She had gotten moving early.

Cal's moment of quiet observation didn't last long before he was spotted from below.

"Hello, up there!" someone shouted from down on the ground. Cal turned his head and saw his wood-chopping buddy waving up at him.

"Good morning!" Cal waved back.

"You better come get you some chow before it's gone!" the man said. Then, laughing, added, "But put on some pants first!"

Cal glanced down and realized he was only a leg shake away from letting the cow out of the barn. He grinned sheepishly and retreated back into the loft for his pants.

When he returned to the window fully clothed he searched again for Ren. He scanned the back porch. No sign of where she went. His eyes returned to the open door. This time, Montana stood where Ren had once been.

Montana stared up at Cal, silently watching him. He made no effort to wave or speak.

Cal shook off the creepy feeling he got from Montana's stare. He leaned away from the window and sat down to lace up his boots.

That guy was a strange one for sure. He had a magnetic charisma about him, but not in a good way.

Down by the fire, someone handed Cal a cup of coffee and a plate of scrambled eggs. He grabbed a piece of bread from a woman's basket as she whisked past him.

Cal approached a group of men who were smoking cigarettes by the fire. He stood near them balancing his dishes in his hands as he ate, trying to look like he belonged.

"This is good bread. What is this, sourdough?" Cal attempted to insert himself in the conversation.

"Yep, baked fresh every day," one guy with tussled brown hair and heavy stubble said over his shoulder.

"What's on the agenda, today?" Cal asked the group. "What do you guys do around here?"

The group parted slightly and let Cal join the circle.

"You ever been on a farm before, bud?" one guy asked.

"What do you think? He sounds like a northerner," grunted another.

The group chuckled.

"Are you suggesting they don't have any farms up north?" Cal asked.

"That ain't what I meant."

Cal waved the remark off with his hand. "I'm here to work. Just tell me what to do."

"Well, for starters, you can—"

The man's instruction was cut short by another voice behind Cal.

"Badger is coming with me today," said Montana.

Cal winced slightly when he heard the voice. Of course it would be Montana.

Cal turned around to see Montana standing behind him. That smug look. Slight smile and half-closed eyes.

"Sounds good. What are we up to?" said Cal, hiding his apprehension.

"I was thinking we might go hunting."

Great, Cal thought. Just what he was hoping for. A secluded hike in the middle of backwoods nowhere with an armed cult leader. Perfect.

"I'm in," he said. "When do we leave?"

"Meet me over by that hiking trail in twenty minutes." As Montana spoke, he pointed off in the distance to the tree line, far off where the meadow turned to dense forest.

Cal followed Montana's index finger to a slight opening in the brush that looked like a trail.

"Alrighty, see you then."

Cal wolfed down his breakfast, and, minutes later, he headed for the tree line where Montana had pointed. When he got there, he was only slightly surprised to see no one but Montana waiting for him.

Montana carried a rifle slung over his shoulder.

"Should we wait for the others?" Cal asked as he approached Montana. He hoped other people would be joining them, but knew it was not likely.

Montana gave no response. He turned and entered the thick brush.

Cal followed reluctantly.

Within a few steps, the green tunnel of forest closed around them. It became difficult to tell which way was which. Matted vines and slippery moss covered every surface of the terrain. The trees above them grew so closely together that the blue sky was barely visible. The dense thicket blotted out even the sun.

Montana marched through the woods at a rapid clip. He jumped from log to log and ducked under vines. He knew the terrain well. The rifle swung side to side on his back as he trotted along.

Cal did his best to keep up, but his lack of familiarity with the woods made it nearly impossible to match Montana's pace.

"Hey man, hang on a sec. I don't know this area as well as you," Cal called after Montana. His shirt was already damp with a mixture of sweat and dew from the encroaching brush. Cal thought he heard Montana chuckle at his plea for mercy.

"I understand you and Ren spent the night together last night?" Montana's deep voice echoed over his shoulder. He slowed his pace so Cal could catch up and respond.

Cal panted, attempting to catch his breath. Tired, but he didn't want to show it. He wondered if that was what Ren did this morning? Told their transgressions to the leader?

Cal said, "She's not your lady, is she?"

"At The Farm, we are not possessive. What's mine is yours." Montana spoke dramatically, pausing on each word for emphasis.

Yep, he's a creep alright, Cal thought.

"So you like to share, eh? How about young blondes? You got a thing for them?"

"Last time I checked, you are the one who spent the night with a young blonde, my friend."

"Maybe so, but I wasn't professing to be her god or whatever it is you consider yourself to be."

Montana cast a glance over his shoulder but kept walking.

Cal saw the annoyance on Montana's face.

They walked in silence for a few minutes.

"So the gloves have come off, have they?" Montana finally said. He had calmed down now. His voice had returned to its usual zen demeanor.

"What are you talking about?" Cal asked. He was fed up with Montana's contrived persona of the peaceful hippie.

Montana froze in his tracks and pivoted to face Cal. The rage flashed up in an instant. It shone in his eyes as he growled at Cal through clenched teeth. "I'm talking about you and your motive for coming here. Now quit bullshitting me."

Montana's words hung in the air. He waited for Cal to respond.

Cal played dumb. "And what motive is that?"

"It's just you and me out here now, bro. Why don't you knock off the act. You think I don't see your type out here? Trying to knock us down. Trying to expose us as frauds somehow. I see you. I see right through you."

"I'm not sure what you mean, Montana. I'm just here to get a break from society. I need the fresh air."

"Yeah right, man. What are you, a reporter? You a cop? I know you've been asking questions. What are you searching for?"

Cal looked away. Should he just come right out with it? Would Montana reveal anything about Willa? He could not stay out here much longer. Every minute he spent at The Farm was a minute lost from his investigation. He turned back to Montana. The cult leader was still staring at him. Rifle on his back, fingering the strap that rested on his bulging shoulder.

"I'm not a reporter or a cop."

Montana relaxed his grip on the rifle strap. "Yeah? What is it then?"

"I'm trying to find a girl. I think she was here not long ago."

"I see. You're one of those hero types. Saving a damsel in distress. She an addict?"

Cal dropped his gaze to the ground. "I think so."

"Don't you know you can't save them, man? If she's using she don't give a shit about you or anyone else. Even if you find this girl she ain't coming home."

"What makes you so sure?" Cal asked.

"I see it every day. Every fuckin' day." Montana's voice showed his exasperation. He had become calloused by the addicts he had seen. "They try to get clean and fail over and over again."

Montana sat down on a rock. He unshouldered the rifle and leaned it against his leg while he drank from a canteen. He offered the canteen to Cal.

Cal shook his head but kept listening, waiting to see if Montana would say more. He wondered if Montana was telling the truth or if this was another part of the act.

Montana became calm again before Cal's eyes. Talking about his flock seemed to soften him up.

Cal said, "Her name is Willa. Does that sound familiar?"

Montana didn't even need to think about it. "Yeah, I remember her."

"You do? Recently?" Cal was excited. His first real break in the case.

"She passed through here maybe a week ago. Said she wanted to stop using. Pills. That was her vice."

"That's right," Cal said. "What else?"

"Couldn't have been more than nineteen years old. Tiny little thing. If I remember right, she lasted about two days before she relapsed."

"Where did she go?"

"I don't know, brother. Where do any of them go? Back to the flophouse I guess. I heard some yahoo picked her up out at the road."

"Does that mean someone saw her leave? Could they describe the guy or his car?"

"You'll have to ask..." Montana trailed off, staring intently in the distance over Cal's shoulder. "Hang on. Don't move. Stay right where you are."

Cal started to respond, but Montana cut him off. "Shhh." He slowly raised the rifle from his leg. The barrel inched upward until the sight was fixed on Cal's boot, then his knee, then his waist. The barrel stopped with the rifle aimed directly at Cal's head. Montana cradled the stock snugly against his shoulder and lowered his eye to the sight.

Cal remained frozen in place, stricken with fear, the rifle aimed at his forehead.

Montana slipped his finger on to the trigger.

Sweat poured down Cal's back. He started to speak, to plead for his life. At that instant, Montana swung the rifle to Cal's left and squeezed the trigger.

Cal dove for the ground and covered his head.

When Cal opened his eyes, Montana looked down at him, laughing. "Dinner is served!" he bellowed. Without waiting for Cal to respond, Montana bounded off in the direction of his rifle fire.

Cal rose to his feet. He dusted himself off and followed Montana, keeping a safe distance between them.

By the time Cal caught up, Montana was already field-dressing the animal carcass.

Cal peered over Montana's shoulder as he worked. The animal was about the size of a large dog but much fatter and had less hair.

"Ugly sucker, isn't he? What is that?" Cal asked.

"Wild pig! Ever had it?" As he spoke, Montana tugged back the hog's head and sliced its throat with one quick motion. Blood gushed from the open wound and pooled on the ground around Montana's knees.

The musky stink of the wild hog and the sight of its flowing blood made Cal a little woozy. He took a step back. "No, can't say that I have."

Montana worked in a frenzy, thrilled with his kill. He knew it would provide enough food for the whole group. He cut two thick branches from a nearby tree and sliced off all the small limbs, turning them into long, smooth poles. He then flipped the hog on its back, laid the two poles lengthwise on the beast and tied them tightly. When he had finished, the pig was strapped into the contraption with the poles extending about three feet past its head and rear.

"That looks like one of those old carts made to carry around kings on the shoulders of peasants," Cal muttered.

"Those old carts are called litters. You should look it up next time you go on the internet. Now grab that hog's butt and let's get moving."

Cal did as he was told.

The two men hoisted the bounty on their shoulders and marched back to the farmhouse covered in the blood of the wild hog they had slaughtered.

15

The pig hung headless, dangling upside down by its feet, the carcass split wide open in the middle. A man and a woman stood before it, slicing knives with razor precision. They removed hunks of flesh and muscle, carefully setting each piece of meat to the side as they butchered the beast.

Montana, still frenzied from his kill, hovered behind the butchers as they worked. He pointed and called out the cuts of meat.

"Shoulder! Loin! Belly!" he exclaimed. "Set that belly over here in this skillet. Have you ever had fried pork belly?" he asked a man next to him who was also observing the slaughter.

"Yes," the man said.

"Not like this you haven't. As wild and fresh as it gets."

Cal had reclaimed his seat by the campfire. Close enough to see and hear Montana, but far enough away so that he could avoid the frenzy. Cal already wore enough of the pig's blood. He didn't need to participate in the butchering.

Ren exited the backdoor of the farmhouse and stepped off the porch. She entered the yard, taking a wide berth around the dangling hog. She spotted Cal by the fire and smiled at him.

Cal smiled back and raised a hand in greeting.

She made her way over to him and pulled up a chair.

"So, how was the hunt?" Ren said.

"Successful," Cal said with a slight grimace.

"I can see that," said Ren, nodding toward the makeshift slaughterhouse. "And what about Montana? How did it go with him?"

"He's…interesting."

"I know. Isn't he great?"

"I could see how someone might say that," said Cal cautiously. "You really like him, eh?"

"Meeting him changed my life. I mean, completely changed my life."

"Yeah?"

"Before I came to The Farm I was living on the streets. My life revolved around pills. Whatever I had to do to get them, I did it."

Cal was quiet for a moment. What Ren described was a pretty serious transformation. He asked, "You came to The Farm and quit, just like that?"

"No, it's not that simple obviously. But Montana helped me find a purpose in life. He helped me see outside of myself. To understand that not only could I help myself, but I could also help others."

"I see," Cal said, being careful not to trivialize Ren's experience. He couldn't help noticing the cultish devotion people paid to Montana around here. It felt a little dangerous. And now Ren was using that same tone, that same unwavering commitment. He needed to tread lightly or risk exposing himself and his doubts.

"Do you *really* see?" Ren asked. "Do you see that I am here to help you now? I am here in this very place at this very moment to help you right now. Do you see that?" Ren's face seemed to fill with light. She gazed into Cal's eyes as she spoke.

For a moment, Cal gazed back at her, pondering her suggestion. Could she be right? Was he in fact fated to be here right now? Maybe he did need help in a way he refused to admit even to himself. Was it possible Ren could look directly into his soul and understand his spiritual needs more deeply than he?

"I need to, uh, I think I need to take a walk," he stammered. "All this blood is getting to me…is there somewhere I can wash it off?"

Ren, still watching him, nodded slowly. "Yes. The creek around back has a deep eddy. We use it for swimming. Come on, I'll take you."

Cal watched Ren run ahead of him through the field. When she reached the woods, she kept running and disappeared into the thicket.

Cal took his time crossing the field. The blood from the slaughtered pig made his shirt hang cold and slick against his chest. He walked slowly after Ren until he reached the forest opening she had entered.

"Hello?" he called into the woods.

He heard water splashing a hundred feet ahead of him and then Ren laughing. "Come on, the water feels great!"

Rounding a corner in the trail, he came upon the

swimming hole in a secluded area below a set of trickling rapids. The cove was surrounded by greenery with exposed rocks piled around the sides. On one of the large rocks lay Ren's dress.

Honeysuckle bush created a natural barrier around the swimming hole. The sweet scent of its small, white flowers filled the air and attracted butterflies and bees to the hidden forest oasis.

As Cal approached the clearing, he spotted Ren treading water in the middle of the pool. Her hair was wet and long, slicked back over her head. Her bare legs kicked beneath the surface of the clear water.

"I was going to say I forgot my bathing suit, but I see that isn't a requirement around here," Cal said as he began peeling off the blood-soaked clothing.

Ren laughed and sent a splash of water over the edge of the pool. She watched as Cal stripped out of his clothes and dipped each item one by one in the water to rinse it clean. He then draped the wet clothing on the rocks near the bank.

"How deep is it?" Cal asked. He dipped a toe in the water, wearing only his underwear now.

"Deep enough."

Cal took a flying leap and landed in the pool a few feet from Ren, sending a wave of water splashing over her. When he surfaced, his head was only inches from hers. The two faced each other, treading water to keep afloat.

"Now doesn't that feel better?" Ren asked.

"Yes, it does. It's exactly what I needed," said Cal.

"See, I do know what you need."

"I missed you this morning by the way. Where did you run off to?"

"I had things to do."

"Oh, you did, did you?"

"I did. And besides you were snoring!" Ren laughed and pushed off from Cal's chest, swimming for the edge of the pool.

Cal chased after her. He caught her from behind and dragged her back into his arms. They stood chest-deep in the water now, Ren facing away from Cal toward the edge of the water. He kissed her gently on the neck. She leaned back against his body. "I'll have you know I do not snore," he said.

She turned her head. "That's what they all say."

"Give me another chance?" Cal smiled and played along.

"I don't know. I'll have to think about it." Teasing him. She spun around in the water and faced Cal, their lips inches apart. She raised her chin and closed her eyes, waiting for Cal to make a move.

Cal leaned in and kissed her again. She pressed her body against his. The stream's current flicked and rolled. The water flowed gently around them as they embraced.

The two lounged on the rocks, drying off in the late morning sun. Their hands touched, fingers gently caressing warm skin.

"Is this where you bring all the new guys?" said Cal.

"Only the cute ones."

"I'll take that as a compliment."

"You should."

"So how does this work around here? Are you allowed to date within the group?"

"Am I allowed? I'm allowed to do anything I want," said Ren with a laugh.

"I meant are we allowed? Is anyone allowed?"

"Sure. Just because we don't do drugs doesn't mean we can't find other means of pleasure."

"No argument there," said Cal. He stretched back in the sun, letting it warm his shirtless chest.

"We all try to get along. It's a big farm but it can be a small place, if you know what I mean," said Ren.

"Not a whole lot of privacy in that house I don't guess," said Cal.

"That's for sure," said Ren. "And word gets around pretty fast." She winked at Cal and turned over on her stomach.

Cal watched her naked legs lazily tossing, knees bent with her heels almost touching her butt. Her underwear was sandy from the dry, loose dirt and so were the bottoms of her feet. Her left hand absentmindedly traced a pattern in the dust next to her.

"It probably gets a little crowded at times. Hard to get away from watchful eyes?" said Cal.

Ren didn't seem interested in Cal's line of questioning. "Yeah, I guess. Everybody is pretty good about taking care of each other."

"Taking care of each other? Is that what Montana meant by sharing?"

Ren laughed. Still lying on her belly swinging her legs above her. "Oh, I don't know about that. Maybe some of the guys get the idea they can be with any girl they want, but us girls don't always share that sentiment. Sorry about their luck."

"But Montana, though. You went to see him this

morning bright and early. You and him have a thing?"

"Are you getting jealous already?" Ren slapped her hand playfully in Cal's direction. "Watch out now. That'll never work with me."

Cal laughed it off. Was he jealous of Montana? Maybe she was right. "That's not what I meant," he quickly said. "I'm just saying, you know, I don't want to come in here and steal the boss man's lady."

Ren rolled over on her back now and laughed out loud. "Oh please! What is this, the nineteen-fifties? You think this is West Side Story?" She kicked her legs out, still laughing, and put her hands behind her head. She lay there watching the water, waiting for Cal to respond. Challenging him.

Cal let it drop. He changed the subject. "Listen, do you remember a girl out here a week or two ago named Willa?"

"Oh, now you're trying to make me jealous? I know that game."

"No seriously. She's just a friend. I was hoping to catch up with her."

Ren was silent for a few seconds. She sat up. "What is it about her? I heard you've been asking other people about her, too."

"I just want to find her."

"Fine. But you need to remember something for your own good. The group doesn't want any trouble. People come out here poking around and asking too many questions, they don't get to stay very long," said Ren, sounding threatening but then softening her tone. "And I like you. I want you to stay." She looked up at Cal, smiling again.

It felt like a warning, but Cal played it cool. "I like you

too." Smiling back at her and holding eye contact. "Just one more question and then I swear I'm done. Montana said Willa got picked up by somebody out at the road. Do you have any idea who picked her up or what kind of car it was?"

Ren sighed. She stood up. Gathered her dress from the rock and slid it over her head. She patted the fabric and smoothed it over her waist and hips. "I remember. I saw her leave."

Cal sensed Ren was done talking but he was almost there. He raised his eyebrows to indicate he was still listening.

"It was a blue car. A Pontiac I think. The guy driving, I'm pretty sure I have seen him before. Larry or Luther or something like that. He's a real piece of shit."

"Thank you, Ren. I really appreciate it."

"Yeah, okay," she said. But the energy was gone from her voice now. "Hope you find your friend."

Ren ducked under a tree branch and disappeared from sight. She headed back toward the farmhouse, leaving Cal sitting on his rock alone by the stream.

From his office on the second floor of the farmhouse, Montana watched Ren crash out of the woods near the swimming hole. She was a hundred yards off, but he knew it was her. That dress clinging tightly to her body, arms swinging as she walked. She was on her way back to the house and she looked pissed off.

"Yeah, I know," Montana said into the phone that was pressed against his face, "I just think we should keep an eye on him."

He stopped talking and listened to the voice on the other end of the line. He tapped his fingers on the wooden desktop. Watched Ren getting closer. Now he could see her features. The tiny little nose scrunched, eyebrows in a knit. She had that frustrated look in her eyes. Stomping her feet as she walked.

That girl is an open book, Montana thought.

"Okay, I won't," said Montana, still talking on the phone. "But I just thought you should know. You might want to put somebody on him. He's asking a lot of questions."

Ren stepped up on the porch.

"Listen, I gotta go. I'll keep you posted."

Montana hung up the cell phone. He slid it in a desk drawer.

Ren's boots stomped up the stairs and down the hallway to his office door. She knocked.

"Montana, are you in there?"

"Yes."

"Well, can I come in?" Still sounding frustrated like she had something she needed to get off her chest.

"You're going to anyway."

Ren pushed open the door and stepped into Montana's office. She stood in the middle of the room staring at him with one hand on her cocked hip.

"Yes?" said Montana.

"What's he worried about that girl Willa so much for?" said Ren.

"Did he bring her up again?"

"Yeah, down at the swimming hole just now. Wanted to know if I remembered her and who picked her up."

"What did you tell him?"

"What do you think? I had to tell him something," said Ren. "He knew she got picked up by somebody. I told him about that dumbass Luther."

"And what did he say?"

"He wants to find her."

"Does he know anything about us?"

"I don't think so. He's just obsessed with that girl is all. He's nosey though."

"True. I don't care if he goes searching for that little tart as long as he gets the hell out of here. We have too much at stake to risk him digging into our business."

"What do you want me to do?"

"Go make nice with him. He seems to have taken a liking to you. I'm going to get some guys together. We'll run him out of here by the end of the day. As soon as I'm sure he's not investigating us."

"What if he is?" said Ren.

"Don't worry about that. We'll deal with it."

"What are you going to do about him?" Ren walked over to Montana as she spoke. Her voice changed as she walked. Getting softer now. Sweeter.

"I said don't worry about it."

Ren stood over Montana now. She lowered herself into his lap, sliding her hips back so her thighs stroked Montana's leg. She reached for one of the drawers slowly, resting her hand on the pull.

"What you got in here today?" She was being coy, asking a question she already knew the answer to. Rhetorically, not asking to get an answer, but instead coaxing him to open the drawer.

Montana slapped her hand away. "Get up. Not now."

Ren stood up, acting hurt. "Fine. But you owe me."

"We'll see. Now go catch him before he starts talking to somebody else."

She spun around and stomped out of the office. Her footsteps receded down the long hall.

Montana turned back to the window. He watched Cal exit the woods in the same place Ren had. He saw Cal gather his bearings and slowly begin making his way across the field back to the farmhouse.

Montana stared at Cal's shape cutting across the open field. He muttered to himself, "Tyson, I don't know what you're doing here, but I don't like it. You better mind your own business. Don't make me do something we'll both regret."

When he was sure Ren had left the hallway, Montana got up and closed the door to his office. He turned the deadbolt and sat back down at his desk. He took the cell phone out and set it on the desk top.

Then, he stuck his hand in the desk drawer that Ren had been fingering. He pulled out a small leather case about the size of a jewelry box. He lifted the lid to reveal several tiny ziplock baggies filled with white powder. He opened one and dumped the contents on his desk.

Leaning forward with a finger over one nostril, Montana snorted some of the powder. He switched nostrils —covering the other one this time—and finished off the pile.

Montana dialed a number on the cell phone. He leaned back in his chair and put his boots up on the desk. "It's me again," he said. "Listen, I need him out of here now." He listened for a few moments. "I hear you and I don't care." Raising his voice, he said, "The last thing we need is somebody out here asking a bunch questions. You of all people know that. I'm running him out today."

He licked a finger and ran it over the desk to pick up the rest of the powder, and then rubbed it on his gums as he listened.

"You do whatever you need to do. My advice is get a tail on him and don't let him out of your sight. Matter of fact, we might even want to find this Willa gal before he does. A little extra insurance, if you get my drift. I think she's been hanging out with that waste of skin, Luther."

Montana paused, listening.

After a few seconds, he spoke again. "In a room at that piece of shit motel in town where the meth heads hang out, I'm sure. Just send somebody over there and watch for her. Is Mack still in town? Why don't you put him on it. I can't be worrying about that bullshit and running this place at the same time. I'm about to have a pig roast. If this Tyson fellow gives me any trouble, he's going on the spit right next to the hog. Now just get it done and let me know when you have her."

Montana hung up the phone. His brain rushed with pleasure from the cocaine. Stars fired behind his eyes. He felt like a god again. He was a god. Now to get this nuisance out of his kingdom.

Ren intercepted Cal as he approached the farmhouse. She talked sweet to him again as though nothing had happened, "What took you so long, hon? I thought you were right behind me."

Cal was starting to wonder about this girl. The way she turned it on and off so easily. It was a little unnerving. And yet again, he noticed she had gone straight into the house after leaving him. Was Montana in there? Was she reporting back to him? Cal was quickly losing trust in Ren, the only person with whom he had made a connection out here. But for now he played dumb. "I thought you were mad at me. The way you stormed off I figured I upset you."

"Stormed off? Oh, no I'm not mad." She tried to laugh it off, but Cal could tell she was forcing it.

Cal's adventure at The Farm was winding down. He could sense it. He'd had about all he could handle of the place. The one lead he had gained on Willa's disappearance was going to have to suffice. It was time to get moving. In fact, he didn't care if he ever saw Montana again.

Ren took Cal's hand. She tried to lift it and pull his arm around her shoulder. She pawed at his waist, hugging him, drawing him in again.

But this time he saw through the ploy.

"What are you doing? Not even twenty minutes ago you wanted nothing to do with me," said Cal.

"No, baby, you got me wrong," said Ren. "Remember, I'm here to help you."

"Help me do what?"

"You know, get clean. Start a new life. That's why you're here. You came to find me." She stared up at Cal. Her bright eyes and soft voice.

Cal felt himself falling for it again. Ren was so attractive with her charisma turned on full steam. She was sucking him back in.

"I did?" Cal asked like a man in a daze. His arms circled Ren's waist slowly. She stood on her tip toes and kissed him.

"That's it. Now you're back. Don't leave me. We need each other," said Ren. "Lunch will be ready soon. The wild pig you and Montana got this morning. Don't you want to taste the fruits of your labor?"

At the sound of Montana's name, Cal snapped out of it. He released his grip on Ren's waist and stepped backward. "No, I need to go. It's time for me to leave now."

Ren reached for him, but he pushed her arms away gently this time. "It's time for me to go." He looked in her eyes and saw defeat in them.

Ren dropped her gaze to the ground. She smoothed her dress with her hands, dragged the toe of her boot in the dirt.

"Are you sure?" she asked.

"I am. This place is not a good fit for me. I can't stay."

The sound of clapping hands echoed across the yard.

Montana stood on the porch of the farmhouse. With his back straight, he surveyed the group like a pastor to his flock. He continued clapping slowly until everyone was quiet.

A small crowd gathered to hear him speak.

"Badger, I could not have said it better myself," shouted Montana over the sound of his own clapping hands.

Ren's body language made it clear something was wrong. The residents of The Farm shifted about uneasily and waited for their leader to continue speaking.

Montana finally stopped clapping. He dropped one hand to his side and raised the other, pointing his index finger directly at Cal. "Just like you said. The Farm is not a good fit for you. And you can't stay."

Cal felt the nerves rising in his stomach. He was a stranger here and he had no friends. Montana, on the other hand, had blind loyalty from the entire group. They would do whatever he told them. Cal knew he needed to make a quick exit. "You don't have to tell me twice. I'm on my way out now," he said.

"Good. Don't ever come back here," Montana shouted with an emotion Cal had not seen from him. Montana was putting on a show for his audience. "Leaf and Jackrabbit, escort him out of here. Take him all the way to the road and make sure he leaves."

Before Cal could respond, the two hippies grabbed him, one on each arm, and began dragging him toward the road. "Hold on a second, I can walk. There's no need for this kind of treatment," said Cal.

But Montana gave no response. He stood on the porch and watched Leaf and Jackrabbit drag Cal away.

The group parted to make room for the three to pass by. The people of The Farm, who only a day before had welcomed Cal with open arms, all stared at the ground, giving no response and showing no sympathy. Cal had been excommunicated. The leader had spoken and his word was final.

Cal shuffled his feet to keep up with his escorts. Neither man said a word the entire walk to the road despite Cal's protests. When they reached the road, Leaf or Jackrabbit—Cal didn't know who was who—opened the gate, and the other guy tossed him out on the road.

Cal walked back to the spot where he had hidden the MG. His investigation at The Farm was over, but he felt sure it was not the last time he would see Montana, whether he liked it or not.

Montana was trouble. His sudden and rough dismissal of Cal was proof of it. Montana did not like anyone poking around his business, and that alone was enough to put him on Cal's radar as a suspicious character.

Cal made up his mind to find out whatever he could about Montana and the commune when he got back to town. For now, he wanted nothing more than a stiff glass of bourbon and a hot shower.

16

"Get up."

Willa opened her eyes. She lifted her head off of the carpet and rolled over. Her shoulder was sore from lying awkwardly on it all night. "What time is it?" she said. Her voice croaked. Lips cracked and dry, needing water.

"Time for you to get your ass out of the way," said Luther. He nudged her leg with his pointed boot.

"Good morning to you, too."

Willa bent her knees to move her legs away from the motel room door. Her eyes focused. She saw Luther standing above her with his hand on the door knob. He was dressed, dark hair slicked back with pomade. "Where are you going?" she asked.

"Out."

"When will you be back?"

"When I get done doing what I'm doing," said Luther. "Why don't you go down and play by the pool again. Think of some more smart things to say. You probably just about used them all up last night."

Memories of the previous night echoed in Willa's head. Those idiots planning the robbery, Luther getting violent, her sleeping on the motel floor. She closed her eyes again and dropped her head back to the carpet.

Luther opened the door and started to leave. As the door closed, Willa extended her leg and caught it with her foot. Through the open crack, she said, "Hey, wait."

She heard Luther's voice from the walkway. "What?"

"Did you leave me anything?" she said.

All she heard were Luther's footsteps descending the metal stairs.

Willa got up off the floor. She did her best to straighten her appearance. In the mirror, she saw red marks on her throat from Luther's grip. She dusted the marks with a little makeup to blend it in.

She surveyed the room. The place was a mess. They had been living in the motel over a week and hadn't cleaned the room once. She picked up the beer cans, emptied an ash tray, made the bed, put away the clothes.

Willa propped open the motel room door to air out the stifling stink of stale beer and cigarette smoke. She stepped out the door and turned to look back into the room, admiring her work. She felt better now after cleaning up. Like she had done something productive. It felt good to have accomplished something.

She stood on the walkway outside her room and gazed out over the parking lot. She put her hands on the metal railing and let the morning sun shine on her face and warm her body. She remembered how good the sun felt yesterday by the pool.

Willa grabbed one of the chairs from her room and dragged it out on the balcony. She left the door propped open behind her. She sat in the chair and put her feet up on the railing.

The muffled street noise—cars cruising by, faraway conversations of people on the sidewalk, ambient sounds of small town life—lulled Willa back to sleep.

She closed her eyes and dozed off.

Across the street from the motel, Mack Abbott lowered a pair of black binoculars from his face. The binoculars had special lenses to prevent them from glinting in the sun, custom-made for discreet surveillance. He picked up a notepad from the passenger seat next to him and jotted:

11:15 a.m. - boyfriend leaves
11:35 a.m. - Willa brings chair out on balcony. Sits in it and appears to fall asleep.

Mack removed a styrofoam McDonald's coffee from the cup holder in his 1995 GMC Sierra and sipped it carefully. His parking spot on the street provided a perfect vantage point from which to watch Willa's and Luther's door on the second floor of the rundown motel.

Some politician on the radio was telling Mack how it was good for the people of Kentucky that coal plants were closing. Didn't they realize coal jobs are dangerous and unhealthy, the politician wanted to know. Not to mention bad for the environment. "Sometimes people need us to step in and help them see the truth by creating new policies," the politician said.

Mack reached for the radio dial and turned it off. He picked up a cell phone and dialed a number.

"Yes?" said the voice on the other end of the line.

"I found her. So far she has barely left the room. The boyfriend took off about half an hour ago."

"Where did he go?"

"Not sure. I figured I should stay with the girl. You want me to get another guy to tail the boyfriend?" said Mack.

"Not right now. Just keep an eye on the girl. Any sign of the private detective from Lexington yet?"

"Not yet."

"Okay, keep your eyes out for him. He's on his way back to town by now, and he will be looking for her. Ideally we get her before he shows up. She's going to make a nice bargaining chip in case this Tyson fellow decides to cause trouble for us."

"Roger that."

"If you see an opportunity to grab her without being spotted, go for it. Otherwise just watch them and report back."

"Okay then."

Mack hung up the phone. He sipped his coffee. Raised the binoculars to his face again.

Willa was still slumped in her chair on the balcony. Eyes closed, her head tilted to the side resting on her shoulder.

Mack scanned the walkway. People coming in and out of rooms. A maid cleaning three doors down.

Too much traffic right now. Too much daylight. Mack settled in.

"You want me clean?"

Willa opened her eyes. The maid stood there with one

hand on her cleaning cart.

"What?" said Willa.

"Excuse. I clean now. You want?" said the maid. She nodded toward the open motel room door.

Willa sat up. She thought about the wreckage in her hotel room, about the drug residue on every flat surface. "No, that's okay," she said.

"You sure, Miss? I don't mind. I clean the room."

"We're fine," said Willa.

The maid pushed her cart on to the next room, muttering to herself in Spanish as she passed by the open door.

Willa stood and dragged her chair back into the motel room. She let the door close behind her. The dark room still smelled musty. She pulled back the curtains and flooded the room with light. Dust particles danced in the rays of sunshine. The clock on the nightstand said 11:57.

Willa sat down in one of the chairs. It had been almost a full day since her last pill. Her skin felt itchy. Her jaw tightened. Beneath the table her leg bounced on the floor with restless energy.

She got up and began scouring the room, searching for a pill. She opened drawers, checked pockets, lifted up the bed skirt. Nothing. Not a single pill anywhere in the place. She felt her stomach tightening with cramps. Sweat beaded up on her forehead. She curled into a ball on the bed, thinking she would lie there and grind it out, pass the time and wait for Luther to come home.

After a few minutes, she got up again and began pacing. "I have to stop thinking about it," she whispered to herself. She decided to take a bath, but thought better of it when she saw the ring of grime around the tub. She took a shower instead. The hot water felt good. It loosened her sore muscles and reduced the cramping in her stomach. By the time she got out of the shower, the craving had subsided and she felt good enough to get dressed and go outside.

Down in the parking lot of the rundown motel, a group of guys lounged in lawn chairs in the afternoon sun. They were listening to music and laughing at each other. Having fun and drinking beers concealed in small paper bags.

Willa leaned against the second-floor railing, watching the men in the parking lot. Her blonde hair was still wet from her shower. She wore a t-shirt and a tiny pair of shorts—her dad would have hated them—that exposed her long, brown legs.

She went back in the motel room to get her sunglasses and a quick spray of perfume. Then, she headed downstairs to the parking lot.

Halfway over to the group of guys she realized one of them was the fat, hairy pervert from yesterday at the pool. Great, she thought, just what I need right now.

As soon as she got within earshot, the men began calling to her.

"Hey, mama, where you going?" said one guy.

"Come on over. I saved you a seat," said another as he crudely dusted off his lap. The group of men laughed loudly.

The laughter subsided quickly when they realized Willa was heading right for them. The men, big talkers from a distance, were at a loss for words when suddenly this sexy young woman was actually standing right next to them.

Willa didn't waste any time. She plopped down in one of the chairs. "Y'all got another one of them beers?"

The men were dumbfounded. They stared at each other nervously.

"Fine. I'll help myself," said Willa. She lifted the lid on a red and white Coleman cooler and grabbed a Modelo Especial from under the ice. "Damn, you all are drinking the good stuff."

She popped the tab and tilted it back. The ice cold beer felt good on her throat. Her mood instantly began to lift.

"Where's your man today, mamacita?" said the fat, hairy guy.

"I don't have no man," said Willa with attitude. She took another swig of beer and belched loudly.

The group of men burst out laughing. Willa had broken the tension. The chatter resumed and soon she became part of the crew, listening to their jokes and drinking their beer.

By two in the afternoon, Willa was feeling nice and buzzed from the beer. The men flirted with her, watched her, but she didn't mind. She was getting free beer and they were mostly behaving themselves.

When three of the guys got up and went into a first-floor motel room, Willa zeroed in on them like a hawk. She could tell they were up to something, most likely drugs. She got up, feeling a little wobbly from the booze, and followed the path the men had taken to the room.

She knocked on the closed door. No answer.

"Hey, open up. What are you all doing in there?" she said.

The door opened a crack. One of the men's faces appeared in the gap. "What do you want?"

As he spoke, marijuana smoke billowed out of his mouth. The sweet smell hit Willa right in the face. "I want that," she said, attempting to inhale the smoke as it dissipated around her.

The man opened the door and let her in. The entire motel room reeked from the weed. The men stood in a circle by the bed, passing the biggest joint Willa had ever seen.

Willa stepped up to the circle without hesitation and accepted the smoking joint. She took two puffs and coughed hard, exhaling smoke in a forceful stream. She passed the joint on and turned to the side, continuing to cough.

"Damn, she don't play!" said one of the guys. They all laughed and continued passing the joint.

Willa sat down on the bed, slowly regaining control over her lungs. When she stood up again, the room had changed to technicolor. Her vision flashed like a strobe light. The voices around her sounded like they were in a tunnel. Her body felt warm, like she was floating in liquid. She smiled and felt the grin spread across her face.

'Dude, she's straight cheesing," said one of the guys. The whole group was stoned now. They all turned to look at Willa.

"I think I might be high," said Willa. She touched her face, feeling the corners of her mouth as if to measure the width of her ever-broadening smile. She started giggling and the laughter quickly spread to the rest of the room.

"Yo, you think?" said one of the guys.

Willa fumbled for the door. The handle appeared to be a mile away. She could see her arm outstretched in front of her. Her hand touched the doorknob. She turned the knob and pulled open the door. The bright sun blasted the room with light and heat. It felt good and warm. Her sunglasses shielded her from the brightness. She stepped into the parking lot.

"Dang, dog, close the door!" one of the guys shouted behind her. Willa barely heard him. She put one foot in front of the other until she had crossed the parking lot. She stopped at the snack machine at the bottom of the stairs. Bought a bag of Cool Ranch Doritos and a honey bun, then climbed the stairs, grinning ear to ear.

Inside her room, Willa fell backward on the bed. She turned on the TV. Judge Judy filled the small screen. It felt good to be lying in bed after spending a night on the hard motel floor. Her body began to relax.

Willa devoured the honey bun and got halfway through the bag of Doritos before she closed her eyes and drifted off to sleep.

17

"Is all you do all day sleep?"

Willa opened her eyes. Lying on the bed where she had passed out earlier. The alarm clock said 3:43. She had been asleep for a couple of hours.

The effects of the pot were mostly gone, but she still felt a little groggy and lethargic. She stretched her arms over her head and touched the headboard with her fingertips. Her legs reached downward, thigh muscles tightening as she stretched.

"Ain't that a pretty picture," said Luther. "What'd you do today for real?"

"Got stoned with the neighbors," said Willa. She knew it would piss him off. That's why she said it that way, so nonchalantly. To poke at him.

"What neighbors?"

"I don't know, those guys who sit down in the lawn chairs all day."

"The Mexicans?"

"I guess. They were nice. They gave me beers and

smoked me out."

"Yeah, I bet you showed 'em your ass and they gave you whatever you wanted."

"Maybe I did," said Willa.

Luther didn't say anything. He took a sandwich out of the brown paper bag he was holding and tossed the bag on the bed at Willa's feet.

"What did you get me?" Willa said.

"A knuckle sandwich," Luther said and then laughed at his own crude joke.

"That's not very funny."

Willa reached down and picked up the bag. She hadn't eaten anything other than the honey bun and Doritos. She opened the bag and peered in. Burger and fries. She sat up on the bed and unwrapped the sandwich in her lap.

Luther sat at the table, watching Willa eat.

After a few minutes he said, "I got us something else, too."

Willa paused and looked at him, a french fry halfway to her mouth. "Yeah?"

"Yeah."

Willa smiled. Her body language changed completely. Her eyes lit up. She started bouncing up and down slightly on the bed. She ate the french fry and clapped her hands together.

"Finish your dinner before you get dessert," said Luther.

He reached into his pocket and pulled out a bottle of pills. Clear orange with a white cap. He shook it and the rattle of pills echoed in the small motel room.

Willa watched with excitement as she polished off the hamburger.

Luther uncapped the bottle and dumped a handful of pills on the table.

"What are they?" said Willa.

"Percocet."

"10 millies?"

"Nah, 7.5 but they'll do the job."

Willa scooted her butt to the edge of the bed. She leaned forward and reached for the table where the pills were spread out.

Luther swatted her hand away. "Nope," he said.

"Why?" Willa sounded like a child who had been unfairly spanked for a sibling's mistake.

"These ain't for swallowing."

"Why not? You got at least two dozen there," said Willa.

"Cause I said so. The only way you are getting this Perc in you is up your nose."

Willa scowled. She crossed her arms and sat back on the bed. "You know I don't like to snort them, though. They mess my sinuses up and make me feel all loopy."

"I don't give a rat's ass. You want it, you snort it."

As Luther spoke he removed a plastic card from his wallet. He placed one of the Percocet pills under the card and slowly pressed the weight of his fist on it until he heard the sound of the pill crushing on the table. He lifted the card, wiped the dust off with his finger, and then used the card to corral the powder and chunks into a pile. He repeated the process twice more, each time crushing the pill into a finer powder.

Willa watched silently from the bed. She hadn't had a pain pill in over a day now. She hated the thought of snorting them, but if that was her only choice, she was going to do it.

When Luther had the pill crushed down to the consistency of baby powder, he dragged the card through the pile once more. This time he separated the pile into four large lines.

"Two for you and two for me," he said.

"I don't want one that big."

"Fine. More for me."

Luther split one of the lines into two smaller lines. He removed a dollar bill from his wallet and rolled it up tightly. He leaned forward with the tip of the bill in his right nostril and snorted the powder until the line vanished. He retightened the bill and passed it over to Willa.

Willa took the tightly-rolled dollar bill between two fingers. She stood up and leaned over the table, placing the bill just below one of the smaller lines.

"Don't exhale or you'll blow the powder off the table," said Luther. "Inhale only."

Willa stuck the bill in her nostril like Luther had. With a quick sniff she sucked the powder up the bill and into her nose. She leaned back and coughed. She handed the dollar bill to Luther and sat back down on the bed.

"It burns," she said.

Luther laughed. "Burns so good."

He leaned over and immediately did another line. He stuck the bill out for Willa again, but she waved it off. "Not yet. Let me see how this one does."

"That's my girl," said Luther.

Willa's throat felt raw and tender from the powder, but her brain came alive with fireworks. The effect of the pill hit almost immediately when snorted. Straight to the brain. Her body went numb. The room around her ceased to exist. She lay back on the bed and felt herself floating toward the ceiling.

It wouldn't be the last line she did that night.

18

A few miles away from Willa's motel room, Cal once again sat in the diner across from the police station, thumbing through the local newspaper.

After leaving The Farm, he had stopped off at the trailer just long enough to shower and change clothes. He needed a quick shot of caffeine, and then he wanted to try the police station again and maybe visit Elroy at the Jefferson Mining Company office.

"You're back?"

Cal looked up from the paper to see Penny smiling down at him. He was glad to see her. Maybe he had even come back to the diner hoping to see her again.

"What can I say, it must be the world-class service," he said with a wink.

She did a slight curtsy and poured him a cup of coffee. "Want something to eat?"

"No, just the coffee today," said Cal.

She finished pouring and started to walk away.

"Wait, don't you want to know if I went to The Farm?"

asked Cal.

Penny stopped and turned halfway back to the table. She lowered her voice so only Cal could hear. "I don't know. Do I?"

"I think so. You strike me as the curious type," said Cal.

Penny glanced around the diner. Cal was the only customer in the place except for a few regulars at the counter. The short order cook clanged away at the griddle in back. Penny took a seat in the booth opposite Cal.

"Did you find her?" she asked.

"Ah, so you do remember," Cal said.

"I don't have all day. I'm on the clock," Penny said, being serious but playful about it.

"I didn't find the girl yet, but someone out there saw her. She had been there."

"And then she left?"

"That's right. A guy picked her up. It's not much to go on, but at least it's something."

"What guy?"

"They said his name is Luther and he's—"

The cook hollered at Penny from the order window. He leaned through the opening with his head sticking out over a plate of french fries. "Penny, order up! No sitting!"

Penny rolled her eyes and shrugged at Cal. "I told you. Gotta go. Glad you got a lead on the case though."

She got up to leave. Cal reached out his hand and caught her arm lightly. "Wait a sec."

Penny paused. She looked down at Cal's hand on hers, waiting for him to say something else.

"Do you, um, I was wondering," Cal stammered, "what is there to do around here anyway?"

"You mean for one person or for two?" Penny asked.

"Two I was thinking."

"Well, there's a bowling alley," said Penny.

"Are you a bowler?" said Cal.

"Not really, but there's a bar attached to it."

"I take it you aren't a drinker either given the, uh…"

"Nope. Gave it up when I got clean. But the bar does have karaoke on weekends. Now that I will do."

"Karaoke, eh. How bout that?" said Cal. "No chance in the world you'd get me up on stage, but I wouldn't mind seeing you give it a go."

"Is this you asking me out on a date?" said Penny. She looked down at Cal's hand, still resting on top of hers.

Cal released his grip and dropped his hand back on the table. He looked in Penny's eyes and smiled. "Yes, I think it is. Tonight?"

Penny looked at her watch. "Kind of short notice, isn't it. I can't do tonight. Babysitters are hard to come by that quickly. Single mom and all."

As soon as the words were out of Penny's mouth she paused. She watched Cal's face, waiting to see if mentioning her daughter would bother him.

"Of course. No problem," said Cal.

"How's Saturday night sound?" Penny said.

"Saturday night at the local bowling alley? Sounds mighty fine to me," said Cal.

"Penny!" shouted the cook again. He banged his hand on the counter for emphasis.

"Good," said Penny to Cal. "Meet you there at eight!" She ran off toward the kitchen and disappeared behind the swinging doors.

Cal finished his coffee, dropped a big tip on the table, and left the diner with a smile on his face.

* * *

Two cruisers were parked in front of the police station across the street. Cal wanted to try the police again now that he had more evidence and a lead to go on.

Behind the desk sat the same cop. Still drinking coffee and reading the newspaper like he had never left. The guy glanced over the top of the paper, sniffed, and went back to reading.

"Excuse me, I think we met the other day," said Cal.

The cop stayed hidden behind the newspaper.

The headline on the front page said "Jefferson Mining Company Investing in Workforce Education."

Cal spoke again, "Listen, we got off on the wrong foot. My name is—"

"I know who ya are, Tyson," said the cop from behind the newspaper.

"You do?"

"Yes, I do. You must think I don't know my business. Stranger comes poking around in town, asking questions, getting everyone riled up, I have to look into it."

"True. I guess you do."

"I reckon if you know Brand you must be okay," said the cop.

"You mean Joe Brand?" said Cal.

"Yeah, Joe's an old buddy a mine. Elroy Taylor told me you're from Lexington, so I called Brand to check you out."

The cop was talking about Joe Brand, a retired police officer from Lexington and also a friend of Cal's. Joe had good connections, and he had helped Cal out on a number of cases.

"Glad to hear that," said Cal. "To be honest, I wasn't

sure Joe would recommend me after the thrashing I gave him at racquetball last week."

The cop gave no response.

"You must know I'm staying with Elroy?" Cal continued.

"You told me that yourself last time you were here."

"Oh, that's right. And I mentioned I'm looking for his daughter, Willa?"

"Yep."

Cal could see this conversation was not going well, so he got right to the point. "I still think she's in danger. I know she's technically an adult, but I believe she is being held captive by a drug dealer. I think the dealer is using her addiction to control her."

The cop folded his newspaper and set it on the desk. "Held captive by whom?"

"Does the name Luther ring a bell? Some kind of street rat, maybe a drug dealer, who drives a blue Pontiac?"

"Got a last name?"

"Not yet, but I'm working on it," said Cal. "I think he's pumping Willa with drugs. Just enough to keep her addicted so she does what he says. He likes having her around and he's using the drugs to manipulate her into staying with him."

"Sounds about right. We see that sort of thing," said the cop. "I don't know of any 'Luther the drug dealer.' Get me a last name, and we can see if he has a criminal record. Maybe put a guy on him, pick him up for questioning."

Alright, now we're getting somewhere, Cal thought.

"I'll see what I can come up with. Thank you."

"Yep."

Cal started to leave but then got another idea. "Say, are

you familiar with The Farm, place about ten miles out of town where they do drug rehab?"

The cop about choked on his coffee. "Drug rehab? Shit. Is that what they claim to do out there?"

"As far as I know. Why?"

"If they do drug rehab out at The Farm then I'm Santa Claus," said the cop.

Cal didn't know how to take the cop's answer. He had his own theories about Montana and The Farm, of course, but now he wanted to hear what the local police had on them.

"What do you mean by that? Do you know more about the place? They have some secrets?"

The cop thought about it for a second. He started to respond but changed his mind. "Nah, if that's what they say, then fine."

"What about that guy Montana? He have a record?"

"You met him?"

"I spent about twenty-four hours out there till they kicked me out and made it clear I was not welcome back. That's how I learned about this guy Luther. He was the last person seen with Willa."

The cop perked up a little. He seemed impressed that Cal had gone undercover and dug up some dirt.

"Between you and me, that guy Montana is a bad apple. I'd stay away from him if I was you," said the cop.

"I could have guessed that much. If he's so bad, why don't you pick him up? Has he broken the law?"

The cop fidgeted with the items on his desk. Straightened the pens, smoothed the papers. He chose his next words carefully.

"I see you have done some research. But your research

is only about half complete. I take it you haven't explored Montana's history yet," said the cop.

"I only just met him, but it didn't take long to realize I don't like him."

"Well, I've known him his whole life and never did like him," said the cop. "But there ain't a thing we can do about it."

"Oh?" said Cal.

"Montana Jefferson is the son of Riley J. Jefferson."

"I don't follow," said Cal.

"Riley J. Jefferson, as in the billionaire who owns Jefferson Mining Company," said the cop.

Cal's jaw dropped. "Oh, now that is interesting. I had no idea. So Montana is a spoiled rich boy. That makes sense."

"You got it. And, buddy, it pains me to admit this but the Jefferson family is off limits in this town."

"Off limits?"

"About eight years ago, we got a call about a horrific accident out on Route 12. We get out there and find a mangled mess of minivan and a family of bodies on the side of the road. Montana is sitting on the shoulder beside his pickup truck, mumbling, all out of sorts. The frontend of his truck is smashed up, but the damage to his vehicle is nothing compared to the van. And I'm telling you, this guy Montana is blind drunk. Can't even hardly stand up, let alone drive. He's hollering about how he just drove up and found them all that way. Face all busted up from where he hit the steering wheel when he crashed. He's dead-to-rights on the aggravated DUI and manslaughter, if not murder. I mean there is no chance he didn't cause this accident."

The cop took a sip of coffee and continued, "Well, we

finally get him in the cruiser and start heading back toward town when a call comes in on the radio that we are supposed to turn around. He's not going to jail. Instead, we're supposed to drop him off at his dad's place." The cop shook his head slowly. "And that was that. The man drives drunk, kills a whole family in a head-on collision, and walks away scot-free."

Cal whistled. "This guy really is untouchable then?"

"A few months later, the Jefferson family makes an offer on 200 acres of land outside of town. Take a guess what gets built on that property."

"Wow. Are you telling me that The Farm is underwritten by Daddy's money as a way to give Montana something to do, keep him occupied and out of trouble?" asked Cal.

"I'd bet my next donut on it."

"I knew something was off about that place. Montana, he acts like he is some kind of god. And the people treat him that way," said Cal.

"Preaching to the choir," said the cop. "Montana is a troubled individual with a lot of power and a bottomless checkbook. If your investigation leads you back to The Farm, I'd suggest you just head on home to Lexington. You get yourself on the wrong side of the Jefferson family, you might not see your hometown again."

Cal swallowed hard. He nodded and thanked the cop for the information.

This case was getting deeper than he expected and fast.

19

The Jefferson Mining Company main office occupied a large, white building on Route 119 a few miles outside of town. Cal had planned to stop by the place to see Elroy. After learning about the Jefferson Mining Company's connection to The Farm, he had a second reason to visit the office. He wanted to explore the building a little, maybe ask around and dig up some dirt.

It was late Friday afternoon by the time he parked the car in the gravel lot. He got out of the MG and stepped back to observe the building. The windows were dark. Cal hoped the office had not closed for the day.

The building looked to be about 5,000 square feet all in —not nearly what Cal expected for a multi-billion dollar corporation. Kudzu vines grew up the white walls, covering the building in a green facade. The overgrown vegetation gave the office an unkempt appearance. Wild and abandoned, as though nature was slowly swallowing the building and reclaiming it into the natural landscape.

Cal turned the brass knob and found the door locked.

He cupped his hands over his eyes and peered into the window but could see nothing through the tinted glass.

He knocked on the door and waited.

The blinds to his left separated abruptly. Through the slit a pair of eyes peered out at him. After a few seconds Cal heard the deadbolt unlock. The door opened a few inches before catching on a chain with a metallic clink.

"Can I help you?" said a woman's voice from behind the door.

"I'm a friend of Elroy's. Stopped by to see if he wanted to have a chat this afternoon," said Cal.

"Elroy who?" said the voice.

"Um, Elroy Taylor. He has been working here for a few decades I think."

"Don't know him," said the voice. The door slammed shut.

The unwelcome response left Cal curious, not to mention a little annoyed. He knocked on the door again until the process repeated. A slit in the blinds, the sound of a deadbolt unlocking, and the door opening a crack.

"Sir, what do you want?" said the voice again.

"I believe I already answered that question," said Cal. "Listen, would you mind opening the door so we can talk like human beings?"

A few seconds of silence. Cal stared into the crack but he could see no one in the darkness behind the door.

The woman said, "Are you with the union?"

"No," said Cal.

"The newspaper?"

"Nope."

"The police?"

"I'm not. What on earth is going on here?" said Cal.

The door closed. But this time Cal heard the chain slide over and then dangle free against the metal.

The door opened. Behind it stood a tiny woman with thick glasses. She waved Cal in and then she immediately closed the door and bolted it behind him.

They stood in a reception area stacked high with filing boxes. The boxes rose as tall as Cal's shoulder in neat rows. What used to be a waiting room was now full of boxes. Even the chairs had boxes piled in them. Barely enough room for Cal and the woman to stand next to each other in the cluttered room.

"A little behind on your filing, are you?" said Cal. He patted the top of a stack next to him and released a cloud of dust into the air. The thick, dark dust smelled like soot. Cal coughed and waved his hand in the air to dissipate the cloud. The palm of his hand was stained black with the dust. He tried to wipe it off on the box, but his hand ended up even dirtier for his efforts.

"What is this stuff?" he asked.

"Coal dust. I can't escape it. It's everywhere I go," said the woman.

"That can't be healthy. To breathe it all day, I mean," said Cal.

The woman shrugged. "Been doing it for forty years and I'm not dead yet."

She looked to be in her sixties. Slightly hunched over from typing at a desk all day. Couldn't weigh more than one hundred pounds soaking wet. A tiny woman, but not frail. She was wiry and tough, She looked like she could just as easily shovel coal as type a memo, even at her age.

"Now who was it you said you're looking for?" she asked.

"Elroy Taylor. Are there more offices in the back?" Cal said.

The woman pushed her glasses up on the bridge of her nose. She leaned back and looked Cal up and down.

"In the back of what?"

"I don't know. Back through that door?" Cal nodded at the only other door in the room.

The woman took off with surprising speed. She wound through the stacks of boxes until she reached the door Cal had indicated. "You mean this door?"

She beckoned Cal to follow her. He gingerly stepped through the stacks, doing his best to follow the same path the woman had taken.

When Cal stood beside her again, the woman swung open the door. She reached inside and flipped a light switch. Dim fluorescent lights flickered overhead and sputtered on.

Cal could see it was a warehouse of some kind. Inside were rows and rows of the same filing boxes stacked high and extending as far back into the warehouse as he could see.

The woman leaned into the dark warehouse and shouted, "Elroy? Is there an Elroy back there?"

Her voice echoed through the cavernous warehouse. No sound came but the ambient hum of the fluorescent lights.

She turned back to Cal. "Looks like your friend ain't here."

"What is this place?" said Cal. "This is the Jefferson Mining Company office, right?"

"What's left of it," said the woman.

"You're the only employee here?"

"Don't you read the newspapers? Coal is dying. People are getting laid off left and right around here," said the woman.

"But isn't there like a corporate office or something? Where is Mr. Jefferson?" said Cal.

The woman laughed. "Oh my," she said. "You think you'll find Riley Jefferson here?" She continued laughing. "Riley J. Jefferson hasn't set foot in this office in years, young man."

"Where is he?" said Cal.

"Probably on a yacht somewhere," said the woman. "Maybe I can help you find your friend, though. You say he used to work here? Taylor?"

"Yes, ma'am. Elroy Taylor. As far as I know he still works here, but I may have gotten the location wrong."

The woman closed the warehouse door. She led Cal over to her desk. Cal removed a box from the chair across from her desk and sat down.

"Make yourself comfortable," said the woman. "I'm Elna, by the way. Let me get this computer turned on." She fumbled around on her desk, clicking the mouse and pressing on the keyboard. "Do you know anything about these contraptions?" she asked.

Cal reached over and pressed the button on the monitor. The screen came to life.

"Oh lord, it's a miracle," said the woman. She sat down and started typing. "Taylor. T-A-Y-L-O-R. First name?"

Cal smiled as the woman pecked at the keyboard. "Elroy," he said.

"Elroy. E-L-R-O-Y," she repeated back as she typed one letter at a time. "Mmmm-hmmm. That explains it," she said, staring at the screen.

"Explains what?" asked Cal.

"Your friend. He did work here. Looks like he forgot to tell you he quit," she said. "When was the last time you talked to him?"

Cal was surprised. "Well, this morning actually."

"Oh dear. That's no good," said Elna.

"What does it say?" Cal asked.

"I'm sorry to have to tell you this, but your friend appears to have a secret. He hasn't worked here for over five years."

"What?" Cal was shocked.

"Says here he got injured on the job seven years ago. Had a couple years of worker's comp litigation that ended in a settlement and he hasn't worked a day since."

Cal sat back in the chair, sending up another cloud of coal dust into the air around him. Why would Elroy lie to him? Was he hiding something?

"You mean he hasn't been coming to work at all?" said Cal.

"Not according to our records."

"What has he been doing all day then?"

"I'm afraid you'll have to ask him that yourself."

"He told me…he told his family that…" Cal's voice trailed off as he searched for the right words. This was a perplexing circumstance he had not anticipated. What did it mean?

"Is there anything else I can do for you, sir?"

Cal was deep in thought. He didn't respond.

"Sir, I say can I help you further?"

"Hm?" Cal snapped out of it. "Oh, no, I don't think so, Elna. You have been very helpful. I appreciate it."

Elna smiled at him and bowed her head. Cal returned

the smile and excused himself, leaving Elna sitting alone again among her stacks of files.

Cal's mind raced as he climbed back into the MG. He had to find Elroy. He had to ask him what the heck was going on.

"Chief, come in. This is Brady. Over."

Officer Brady waited for the chief to respond on the radio. He watched in his rearview mirror as Cal Tyson unlocked the silver MG outside of the Jefferson Mining Company main office.

"This is the chief. Come on back," said the reply on the radio.

"Chief, I'm out here on Route 119. I just passed the Jefferson Mining Company office and I saw our buddy from Lexington leaving the building. Thought you might want to know," said Brady.

"What's he doing out there?"

"Can't say for sure. He just happened to be walking out as I was driving by."

"He moves fast."

"What's that, chief?"

"Nevermind. Is he alone?"

Brady looked in the rearview again. The MG was far behind him now. "Appeared to be. Want me to pull him over and find out?"

"No, that's okay for now. Thanks for letting me know," said the police chief. "Do me a favor and keep me posted if you see his car again."

"10-4," said Brady. He hung up the radio and looked back once more.

The MG had disappeared from view.

The police chief stood up from the front desk. He stretched his arms and went back into his office. Once there, he pulled the blinds and closed the door. After a few seconds, he picked up the phone and dialed a number.

"Hello," a voice answered.

"Is he in?" said the police chief.

Silence on the other end of the line. The chief waited. After a minute, he heard someone fumble with the phone and pick it up.

"Hello, chief, what can I do for you?"

"Mr. Jefferson, I won't take much of your time. Wanted to let you know Cal Tyson visited your office on 119 today."

"Well, now, chief, talking to you is never a waste of my time," said Riley J. Jefferson, his voice strong and confident with a slight southern drawl. "What do you suppose he was doing there?"

"We aren't sure. He was seen leaving a few minutes ago."

"That is curious," said Jefferson. "First he goes after my son and now he's investigating my business. Chief, I think you and I both know this man is becoming a nuisance to our town."

The chief didn't respond at first. He tapped a pen absently on his desk. He said, "Mr. Jefferson, the guy hasn't actually done anything illegal yet."

"First of all, it's Riley. You can call me Riley. I like to think we're friends, aren't we?"

The chief grunted assent.

"And second of all, let's keep in mind the best interests of our town. I'm sure you know an outsider coming in and stirring everyone up, investigating wild goose chases, harassing the biggest employer in the county, now that wouldn't be good for anyone, would it?"

The chief did not respond.

Jefferson continued, "That's what I thought, chief. We want to keep his hands out of our pockets. The less excitement around here, the better. Now, I don't want to tell you your business, chief, but I think an outside agitator such as this Tyson fellow could be run out of town for any number of reasons."

"We will keep an eye on him," said the chief.

"Good. Now see how easy that was? Thank you, chief, for the phone call. And for all the good police work you have done over the past fifteen years," said Jefferson. "Fifteen years…why, that almost makes a career, doesn't it? You hang in there a few more years and you can retire a happy man. Don't do anything to mess up that track record, chief. Goodbye now."

The chief heard the line click dead. He hung up the phone and sat motionless at his desk, staring at the office door.

Phones rang in the outer office, a fax came in on the machine. The clock on the wall ticked.

The chief didn't move from his chair.

20

That evening at the Sunshine Trailer Park, Elroy Taylor sat at the kitchen table waiting for his wife to serve dinner. His cane leaned against the chair next to him. His elbow rested on the table, fingertips of his right hand gently encircling a can of Pabst Blue Ribbon from which he periodically sipped.

Cal watched Elroy closely. He studied Elroy's eyes as they stared off into space somewhere near the middle of the wooden table.

Cal heard Debra preparing dinner behind them in the kitchen. Pasta, tomato sauce, garlic—the aroma filled the trailer. Steam from the large pot of boiling pasta humidified and heated the room.

A thin screen door was all that separated them from the wild nature surrounding the trailer park. Crickets hummed the soundtrack of the rural summer evening.

"Remind me, Elroy," said Cal, "how long have you all lived here?"

Elroy continued to stare into the middle distance as he answered, "Almost twenty years now. We bought the trailer two months before Willa was born."

"That was the *first* trailer, E.T.," said Debra from the kitchen. She called him E.T. sometimes for his initials.

"That's right. We had a starter trailer before we got the doublewide. We've been in this one for thirteen years."

Elroy made no move nor did he change his gaze. His blank eyes stared straight ahead. He took a sip of beer.

"That was when you got your promotion at the mine, right? When you upgraded?" said Cal.

Elroy nodded.

"The mine has been good to you, hasn't it?" said Cal. "A long, fruitful career. It has allowed you to provide for the family for what, over twenty years now?"

Elroy stirred in his chair. He broke his trance like a man who had just awakened from a deep sleep. He slowly blinked his eyes and looked up at Cal in the chair next to him. A slight confusion in his eyes seemed as though he had just realized Cal's presence.

Elroy shifted his eyes from Cal to Debra. "Debra, get Cal a beer, would ya please, hon?" said Elroy.

"No thanks," said Cal. He held up a hand to Debra to indicate he was fine.

"PBR not good enough for you?" said Elroy.

"No, it's not that. I like PBR just fine," said Cal. "It's just that..." Cal trailed off, thinking about how to ask the tough question he knew needed to be answered. "It's just that, well, Elroy, I need to ask you a question and it's not an easy question to ask."

Elroy sat up straighter in the chair. A puzzled look clouded his eyes. He steeled himself, preparing for whatever Cal was about to say.

In the kitchen, Debra removed a tray of garlic bread from the oven. Metal on metal as she laid the tray on the stovetop burners. She took off her oven mitts and leaned on the formica countertop. "Cal, what is it? Did you learn something about Willa?" she asked.

"Not about Willa exactly. Well, maybe," said Cal. "The fact is I'm not quite sure what it's about, but it's a question that bears answering because I think it might be relevant."

There it was. He had started the conversation. No going back now. He had to ask.

"Spit it out, boy. Supper's getting cold," said Elroy.

"Forgive me for adding more trouble to your life in the midst of all this," said Cal, "but it has come to my attention that you no longer work for the mine. And haven't for several years."

Cal delivered his statement and sat back, watching for Elroy's reaction.

Elroy sunk back into his chair. He reached for his cane. Grabbed the handle and started to stand up. Then he sat back down. He placed both hands on the table in front of him. Removed his glasses, wiped his face with a handkerchief, and replaced the glasses on his face.

"Debra, honey, why don't you come over here and sit down," he said.

Debra pulled out a chair and took a seat next to her husband.

Elroy reached his hand across the table and cupped it over hers. He looked like a man much older than his physical age. At only 51 years old, Elroy Taylor had already lived a long, hard life full of grueling manual labor and disappointment.

"Cal, you're right," he said finally. "It has been quite some time since I set foot on the property of Jefferson Mining Company."

Debra exhaled. "Honey, what is this now?" she asked.

Elroy covered his face with his free hand. He hunched over the table and began to cry. His left hand still gripped the hand of his wife. For what felt like minutes, Elroy sobbed into his hand.

Debra waited patiently for an explanation, trying to console her husband.

"It's okay, Elroy. It's okay. Tell us what's wrong," said Debra.

"I never wanted to lie to you," Elroy managed to stammer, his lower lip quivering as he spoke. "It just happened and then I meant to tell you that day, but the timing was never right. The next day I tried again but couldn't find the words. And after a while it became too hard to even think about."

"Tell me what, honey?" said Debra. She looked over at Cal.

Cal could see she was getting uncomfortable.

"What happened, Elroy? Do you," she swallowed hard, "do you know something about Willa? Did something happen with Willa?"

Elroy began crying all over again.

Debra turned to Cal now. "What is it, Cal? Did something happen to Willa?"

Cal looked back at Elroy. "Elroy, can you tell us what happened?"

Elroy blew his nose in his handkerchief. He took a few deep breaths and gathered himself together.

"It was seven years ago," he said. "You know, when I had my injury."

"Yes, when they gave you the office job," said Debra.

"Just let me finish, hon," said Elroy. "Back when I had

the injury, they told me I could never work in the mine again on account of the leg. It would always be dead weight dragging behind me. Well, you remember, we asked them about an office job. Something I could sit at a desk and do, so I wouldn't have to move around on it."

Debra nodded, still holding Elroy's hand.

"I told you they said yes. Honey, I wasn't truthful with you. The truth is I never even asked. The office jobs were being cut even back then. I knew if they gave me a job in the office somebody else was going to get laid off in order to do it. All those young guys, with their families, the thought of putting one of them out of work? I just couldn't do it."

"But what about our family? You had a twelve-year-old daughter then. And a wife," said Debra.

"That's just it, though, I had another option. Since it was an injury on the job, the union rep told me I could file a claim and get money for it."

"A worker's comp claim?" said Cal.

"That's right. I didn't want to put another man on the street and I had this other option in my back pocket. So I did it. I filed the claim."

"What happened?" said Debra. She and Cal were both listening intently, giving Elroy their full attention.

"There was an investigation. They found my injury was directly related to the mine accident, which we already knew. After the investigation, the company came to me with a settlement offer. All I had to do was sign a paper and they would put aside enough money for me to draw the equivalent of my salary every month until I die."

"The paper you signed, what did it say?" said Cal.

"Hell, what difference did it make? The equivalent of

my salary every month for life? And me with this bum leg?" Elroy tapped his dead leg for emphasis. "You better believe that paper was as good as signed. Anyhow the union rep looked it over, and he said it was a good deal. Something about how I couldn't sue them or talk to the media about the accident or the settlement. A small price to pay to take care of my family for life."

When he finished talking, Elroy wilted. He looked exhausted physically, but a renewed light in his eyes indicated that a weight had been lifted from his shoulders.

"Elroy, honey, why didn't you tell me?" said Debra. "You have kept this a secret for seven years? Getting dressed every day and leaving like you were going to the office. With you telling me you were off to work. Why do that to yourself? Why do that to me?"

"Debra, I'm sorry. I am so sorry. Like I said, I never wanted to lie. It just kind of happened and then I couldn't undo it. How could I raise our daughter with her knowing her dad was a welfare deadbeat? How could I look myself in the mirror? And you, could you even respect a man who didn't work? A loser like me?"

"Oh, you stop that right now," said Debra. "You are my husband and I love you. Injury or no injury, job or no job. Anyway, a worker's comp settlement is not welfare. The mining company owed you. You gave them your leg. You earned every penny of that settlement. That's a man who took care of—who takes care of—his family."

Elroy's eyes welled up with tears again. Overcome with emotion, he could not speak. He just gripped the hand of his wife and smiled as the tears rolled down his cheeks.

Cal's mind raced. Elroy's confession wasn't as bad as he had feared. It seemed like a reasonable explanation and the emotions were certainly real. But a seven year lie? And to his closest loved ones. Every morning re-telling that lie as he dressed and left the trailer. What was he doing out there every day? What other details might Elroy be concealing?

There were more questions to ask, but Cal could see the Taylor family had had enough for one night. He backed off and let the couple have some time alone to discuss Elroy's confession.

Hours later, after the dishes were washed and put away, and the lights in the trailer had been turned off for the night, Cal lay in his room thinking about the case.

He had several threads, but so far none of them led anywhere. First, there was Montana Jefferson, the maniacal cult leader with a bottomless checkbook and a direct connection to the local coal industry. And then there was Luther, the greasy drug dealer with a bad reputation. Could they be connected somehow? Willa had been seen with both men over the past few weeks. Was it merely a coincidence or might there be a deeper connection?

A twig snapped outside of Cal's bedroom window. His senses went on high alert. He sat up in bed and held his breath, turning his ear to listen.

He heard it again. This time with the distinct sound of a footstep. Someone was lurking around outside the trailer.

Cal slipped out of bed and stalked quietly over to the window. He placed a shoulder on the wall and inched around until he could see through the glass into the darkness.

At this time of night, a lone telephone pole in the center of the trailer park provided the only light. Cal could see the gravel road that snaked through the park. At the top of the pole, near the light, moths swarmed so thick that at times the light appeared to be covered with a cloth.

Cal pressed his face to the glass, straining to see anything in the darkness. Nothing. The noise he had heard was gone. Maybe it was just his imagination.

Just as he began to relax, a fist raised to the glass right in front of his face. Thick knuckles rapped firmly on the window. Cal fell backward into the bedroom. He stumbled over the bedpost and landed on his butt with a thud.

A peal of laughter came from just outside the window followed by another knock.

Cal regained his composure. He stood up, dusted himself off, and returned to the window. He unlocked the clasp and raised up the sash. The bedroom flooded with the chirp of crickets. Two feet away, still grinning from the fright he just given Cal, stood Eddie.

"You shoulda seen your face, man," said Eddie. "You scared or something? You think I'm here to get you?"

The air stunk of cigarette smoke. Eddie exhaled a white cloud of it as he spoke. He gestured toward Cal's face with the glowing ember of the cigarette.

"What are you doing out there?" said Cal, trying to calm his nerves.

"Looking for you I guess. It's not the first time I ever knocked on this window late at night," said Eddie with a wink. "Come on out here and talk to me. Bring a couple of Elroy's brews with you."

Cal closed the window. He put on his shoes and exited the bedroom. He grabbed a couple of beers from the refrigerator and stepped out the trailer door to meet Eddie.

Eddie was waiting for Cal by the ramp. He accepted the

beer. Popped it and took a long swig, then lit another smoke. "Come on," he said through his teeth with the cigarette still in his mouth. He tossed his head in the direction of the road and started walking.

Cal opened his Coors and followed Eddie.

"I thought about what you said the other day," Eddie said as they walked. Gravel crunched beneath their feet, the only sound in the trailer park other than the chirping insects. "About Willa running away."

"Yeah?" Cal took a drink of beer and listened.

"I don't think she ran away. She's still around."

"You know that for a fact?"

Eddie didn't respond at first. He stopped and turned toward Cal. The street light cast a shadow over Eddie's face. The pomade in his black hair shone with an iridescent hue.

"I asked around," Eddie finally said.

"And?"

"I guess maybe I didn't want to know. Cause I already had an idea about what she was doing."

"Is it bad?"

"She's running around with scum now, man. Real low-lifes. God knows what she's got herself into."

"Do you know where we can find her?"

"If what I heard is true and she's with Luther, then she's probably at that piece of shit motel in town. The one with the pool in the parking lot. That place is nasty. All the meth heads and pill-poppers hang out there."

There was that name again, thought Cal. Luther. It had to be the guy.

"Why don't you go get her?" said Cal.

"Nah," Eddie said slowly. He took a long drag from his cigarette. "You ain't just going to talk someone out of the slums like that. She's gone, brother."

"Just like that? You're giving up on her?" said Cal.

"You don't know these drugs, man. It ain't a choice. Once it takes hold, you're gone."

Cal and Eddie stood in silence for a few moments. Sweat beaded up on their skin from the thick humidity even in the middle of the night.

"You ever heard of The Farm?" asked Cal.

"Everybody around here has."

"Willa was out there recently. She was trying to get clean."

"Sheeyit. If she was trying to get clean that's the last place she should go."

That got Cal curious. "Huh? I thought The Farm was some kind of rehab center," he said.

"Man, you don't even know what you don't know," said Eddie. "You're about to get yourself in shit so deep you can't breathe."

"What do you mean?"

"You remember how I said me and Willa used to steal the pills and sell them?"

"Yes."

"Well, guess who was my biggest buyer."

"Surely not," said Cal.

"Yep. Montana Jefferson himself. That dude has the biggest stash house in this county."

Cal blinked. He shook his head.

"You know what? Somehow that doesn't even surprise me much," said Cal. "I hated him from the minute I met him."

"You went out there?"

"I was trying to find Willa."

"Did you spend the night?"

"Why?"

"I don't know, I've always heard they do weird shit out there."

"Weird like how?"

Eddie shrugged. "Weird like they crush up the pain pills and mix it in the food. Keep a low dose of narcotics in all of the members to keep them mellowed out and happy. I wouldn't put it past Montana, knowing him."

Cal thought back to his time at The Farm. He remembered the trance-like state he entered while listening to music by the campfire, and also the strange pull he felt toward Ren, the way she could manipulate him with her eyes. Could it be that he was drugged?

"Sure would be a good way to guarantee an unlimited supply of free labor," Eddie continued. "Try to leave and, guess what, your body goes into withdrawal. Either you run right back to The Farm where you felt safe, or you relapse and probably end up back there in recovery anyway."

Cal steadied himself against a nearby trailer. He set his beer can down on the bumper and turned back to Eddie.

"You think this Luther guy has Willa at some sleazy motel?"

"Probably. But I'm telling you, man, you're wasting your time. That girl is gone."

"We'll see about that," said Cal.

"How bout another beer, bud?" Eddie said.

Cal didn't hear him. He turned and walked back to the trailer with his mind full of ideas, anxious for first light, ready to continue the search with renewed vigor.

21

"Goddamn, son. What the hell happened in here?"

That's what Merle said when Luther opened the door on Saturday evening about 7:00 p.m. The motel room was trashed. Beer cans strewn all over the floor. Clothes scattered about. A layer of white powder covered the small table top along with several rolled up dollar bills.

Merle dragged his finger across the table and inspected the white residue. He tasted it. "What y'all got into? You started the party early?" he asked Luther.

Luther shrugged.

"Fuck's wrong with her?" Merle asked, nodding at Willa. She lay on the bed with a pillow squeezed tightly over her head.

"She don't feel good."

"I can see that. Don't tell me you pillheads been up all night and day snorting Lortabs," said Merle. "We got a job to do tonight."

"We're fine," said Luther.

"The hell you are. I can see it in your eyes. You're

strung out and that broad can't even stand up. I don't know why I trust junkies. Every damn time they fuck me."

"I said we're fine. She'll be fine," said Luther. "Maybe we should eat something though."

Merle looked at Randy and Jandy who had entered the room behind him. "Get these clowns a Big Mac or something, will you? We need to sober them up a little."

Randy and Jandy turned to go.

"And a Cherry Coke," Willa said from beneath the pillow.

Merle looked back at Randy. "And a Cherry Coke for the princess."

Randy and Jandy left the motel room.

Merle swept empty beer cans off the chair so he could sit down. He blew on the table and a cloud of powder whisked off on to the floor.

"Hey man," said Luther, perturbed. He lunged for the cloud as though he could catch the dust in his hands.

Merle shook his head. "Don't you worry, pal. With the score we get tonight you can buy as much of that crap as you want."

He took a piece of paper out of his pocket and unfolded it on the table. "I never understood the point of snorting pills anyway. If I'm putting something up my nose, it's speed, man. Uppers. Now that shit'll get you going. Make you want to party all night. Make you feel like you can do anything you want."

Luther didn't say anything. He was sitting on the bed, breathing from his mouth and staring dumbly at the table.

"See what I mean," said Merle. "You look like an imbecile sitting there breathing out your mouth. You got any brain cells left in there? How do you expect to rob a room full of people if you can't even get your head out of your ass long enough to look at this here map?" Merle tapped his finger on the paper that was now spread out before them.

Luther shook himself out of the fog. "Huh? Did you say you got some coke?"

"Get your head in the game, boy." Merle slapped Luther across the face. Not too hard, just enough to piss him off.

Luther raised his hand to his face, rubbing his jaw. He glared at Merle.

"There you go. You finally woke up. Look alive, now," said Merle. "And you over there, blondie. Get your butt up and listen to me. I'm about to make you both rich."

Willa rolled over to face them. She still wore the same clothes from Friday. Her makeup was a mess. Mascara streaks on her cheeks, eye shadow looking like she had two black eyes. She lifted the pillow off of her head and sat up.

"Damn shame to see a pretty girl like you falling apart," said Merle.

Willa scowled.

"Okay, then. Now that we're all reacquainted and feeling happy," said Merle. "This here is a map of the bowling alley. Soon as the twins get back we'll lay out the plan."

Willa dropped back on the bed. Her head pounded. Her skin crawled and itched. She placed the pillow back over her face to block out the light.

"Don't you pass out on me. We have important business to discuss," said Merle. "Here they come now. I hear them stomping up those rickety stairs."

The motel room door opened. Randy and Jandy

stepped inside carrying two McDonald's bags. Randy handed a bag to Luther.

Jandy walked across the room to where Willa sat on the bed. He handed her the other fast food bag.

Willa reached up to take it from him. "Are you really twins?" she asked.

Jandy froze. His eyes became frantic. He swiveled his head toward Randy and Merle.

Randy said, "He don't talk."

Willa took the bag. She scrunched up her eyes like she wasn't sure how to take that announcement.

"What my associate is trying to say," said Merle, "is his brother is not the loquacious one of the pair. And, yes, they are twins."

"He don't have no tongue. Born that way," said Randy. "You need to ask him a question, you can ask me. I always know what he's thinking."

"Creepy," said Willa. "Where's my Cherry Coke?"

"They ain't got Cherry Coke at that one," answered Randy.

Jandy still hovered over Willa, watching her bite into the sandwich.

"Tell him to go stand over there, will you?" said Willa to Randy.

"He hears just fine," said Randy.

"Okay, then. Go stand over there. Please," Willa said to Jandy.

Jandy retreated back to the table by his brother. He stood there by the wall, head down, staring into the filthy carpet.

Merle waited for all of the commotion in the room to stop. The place fell silent except for the rustle of cellophane from Willa's and Luther's wrappers.

"Now, where was I?" said Merle. "Oh yeah, I was about to make us all rich."

Cal hadn't been to a bowling alley in years. Even longer since he had set foot in a karaoke bar. He parked the MG in the lot and sat there for a minute collecting his thoughts, trying to transition his mindset from private investigator to date night.

He certainly did not expect to be going on a date in the middle of this case, but hey, since the opportunity arose, why not. A little R and R on Saturday night and then get right back to business on Sunday morning. Go to the motel Eddie had mentioned. Find the blue Pontiac. That was his next move. If he could find Luther he would be one step closer to finding Willa.

He checked his hair in the rearview mirror, brushed himself off a little, and got out.

The sky overhead was darkening, but no sign of clouds. He left the top down on the MG and went inside.

The sound of crashing pins greeted Cal as he entered the electronic sliding doors of the bowling alley. Dim lighting. The smell of cigarettes and the aerosol deodorizing spray used on rental shoes. The carpet glowed with assorted shapes and designs. Noises, lights, colors, scents—the whole scene had the disorienting effect of a Vegas casino.

A couple of kids zoomed past Cal as he stood in the doorway. He stepped aside to let them pass, leaning against the front counter to avoid being run over.

"Evenin', sir. What size?"

Cal turned to greet the front desk clerk. The kid looked to be about seventeen. Pimple-faced, glasses, voice cracking as he spoke. His hands were poised on a pair of size elevens.

"What's that?" said Cal, caught off guard.

"I say what size shoe do you need? Or do you have your own?" said the kid.

"Oh, I'm not bowling. Just here for, uh, which way is the bar?" said Cal.

The clerk pointed to Cal's right. "All the way down on the end."

Cal nodded and headed that direction.

"Excuse me, sir. Just for fun, are you an eleven? It's a little game we play, see who can guess the most people correctly."

"Twelve," said Cal.

"Dangit," said the kid. He slapped the counter in frustration.

"Don't quit your day job just yet," said Cal.

To get to the bar, Cal had to walk the length of the lanes. He watched the bowlers as he walked. Some families, a few small groups of friends. Dancing and bobbing to the loud pop music that blasted through the speakers. The lanes were just about full. The bowling alley was the place to be on Saturday night.

As Cal approached the door marked 21 AND OVER ONLY, the sound began to change. The pop music on the loudspeakers in the bowling alley clashed with the sound of karaoke music inside the bar. With each step, the music became more Classic Country and less Top 40. When Cal pulled the bar door open, he was hit with the full effect of Karaoke Night.

The guy on stage wore blue jeans and a snap-button western-style shirt. His Redwing boots tapped the time on a raised stage as he sang Waylon Jennings into the microphone.

Cal's eyes adjusted to the even darker bar. He scanned the place for Penny. He spotted her in a corner booth and cut across the bar toward her table.

"That's an awfully big booth for such a little lady," Cal said in his best John Wayne voice.

Penny raised her chin and smiled. She looked a lot different than she had in her waitress uniform. Cal barely recognized her. Her brown hair was straight and soft. Not much makeup at all. Just enough to accent her features.

As she scooted around the corner booth to let Cal in, he could see she wore a blue top with thin straps. Low cut, with a string in front just above her chest. Her jeans were light blue and skin tight. Good and worn in all the right places. Under the table, Cal noticed a pair of cowboy boots made from brown, worn leather. She looked good. Comfortable and classy.

Cal sat down in the booth. He pointed under the table at her boots. "Where can I get a pair of those? I'm feeling a little out of place around here."

Penny laughed. "I think you'd look hot in a pair of boots. We'll have to see what we can do. But I don't think these ones will fit you."

Cal smiled.

Penny smiled back.

The karaoke singer finished up his song.

"I have to admit that guy isn't bad at all," said Cal. "The last time I went to a karaoke bar I left with a headache."

"You just haven't been to the right place then," said Penny. "Don't worry, by the end of the night you will be on stage doing a show of your own."

"There's not enough bourbon in this bar."

Penny laughed. "Speaking of which, why don't we get you a drink. Get you nice and lubed up for your performance."

Cal hesitated. "Are you sure?" he asked. "I don't want to make you uncomfortable. I mean, I know you're not drinking."

"That's sweet of you, but don't worry about me. I have been sober for over three years. There is plenty of fun to be had tonight with or without alcohol." She had a twinkle in her eye as she spoke.

Without hesitation, she waved down a cocktail waitress. "I'd like a Sprite with a twist of lime, and he'll have a—" Penny looked at Cal, sizing him up, deciding what to order for him. "He'll have a Kentucky Mule."

Cal raised his eyebrows as the waitress walked away. "Kentucky Mule, eh?"

"You'll love it. Bourbon and Ginger beer with a mint garnish."

"Sounds delicious," said Cal. "So you come here a lot?"

"Not as much as I used to, but sometimes, yeah. There isn't a whole lot to do around here in case you haven't noticed."

"Except for bowling and karaoke," said Cal.

"You got it."

They were silent for a few seconds.

The DJ announced the next singer. A woman made her way to the stage and took the microphone. The first notes of Loretta Lynn's "Coal Miner's Daughter" played on the speakers.

"I can't imagine anyone getting up there to sing stone-sober," said Cal.

Penny tapped her boot to the song.

Cal could feel the vibration under the table.

"You'd be surprised what you can do if you put your mind to it. Good, clean living is more fun than you might think," she said. "Besides, I've got my daughter at home with me now. I would never do anything to jeopardize that."

Penny looked at Cal, watching him again to see how he would respond to the mention of her daughter.

"And you are a good mom for it," said Cal.

"Thanks. Let's change the subject," said Penny. "Tell me more about you. You're here for work. I know that much. Got any family around here? What do you think about our little town?"

Cal told Penny about the Taylor family and about Willa's disappearance. He explained how he was trying to help find her, get her back on the right track before it was too late.

Penny listened to the story, interjecting tidbits about her own past when a detail from Willa's life rang true for her.

Cal finished his Kentucky Mule and ordered another. The two gradually became more comfortable until they were talking and laughing like old friends. Touching each other's legs and arms as they spoke, all the while being serenaded by the hits of old-time country music. They sat in their dark corner booth and flirted like a couple of teenagers as their surroundings slowly faded away.

"This here is the main entrance. Big, automatic double glass doors," Merle said to the group at the motel room. He stood over his hand-drawn map of the bowling alley.

Randy, Jandy, and Luther gathered around him, listening.

Willa sat on the bed, only mildly interested.

"You got entrances on both sides of the building, here by lane 20 and then all the way down on the other end at lane 1." He tapped the map with a thick index finger to mark the exits. "So that's three doors total. Do you follow me?"

He stopped and looked at each of the three men to make sure they were paying attention.

They nodded in agreement.

"What about you, little miss, how many doors?" Merle said to Willa.

"Three," said Willa from the bed. She was half-listening to Merle's pitch, half-watching the television.

The TV was showing an infomercial about a high-powered juicer that could handle any fruit or vegetable you stuff into it.

"Alright then. Good," said Merle. "Now, I'm sure you are wondering who goes where. Don't worry, Merle's got that all figured out, too." He paused to take a drink from his flask. "I'm taking the front door. The main cash register. Once I get it situated, I'll be watching the side doors. From that front counter I'll be able to see all three exits."

"What about us?" said Luther.

"Hold your horses. I'm getting to it," said Merle. "I want Randy on the right side door and—"

"Our right or your right?" said Willa. She was staring at the juicer on TV, watching it blend up whole apples, core and everything.

"The east side of the building," said Merle, a little perturbed.

"Bet you five dollars you can't tell us which way is East right now," said Willa. She was messing with him, having some fun at his expense.

"Well, you little…East is over that way," said Merle pointing toward the bathroom.

"You sure?" said Willa.

"The goddamn lane 20 door. That's where Randy comes in," said Merle.

Willa smiled, still staring at the screen.

Merle collected himself and went back to describing the plan. "Jandy comes in the lane 1 door." He glared at Willa to see if she would make a smart comment. When she gave no response, he continued, "And Luther, you and Willa, come in with Jandy. That will put you right next to the bar. Once Jandy gets started working the lanes, you slip into the bar and do your thing."

"Do we get guns?" said Luther.

Merle nodded over at Randy. The two brothers left the room. They went out to the trunk of the car and came back with a duffle bag.

Jandy laid the duffle bag on the bed and Randy unzipped it. The bag was filled with guns. Five shotguns and a half dozen handguns. Merle took the weapons out one at a time, handing a shotgun to each person like he was

Santa Claus on Christmas morning. When he got to Willa, he said, "Can you handle one of these things or is it too heavy?"

"I'm not taking a fuckin' gun in there with me. Armed robbery? That's like a felony," said Willa.

"You're gonna have a hard time convincing someone to give you their money without one," said Merle.

Willa turned her attention away from the television for the first time. She looked around the room at the men, all of them holding shotguns. She swallowed. This plan was about to get real, whether she liked it or not.

Willa leaned forward and reached into the duffle bag. She shifted the guns around until her hand rested on the grip of a SIG Sauer 9mm. She removed it from the bag, held it up and pointed it toward the television.

"Armed and dangerous," said Merle. "Hey, that thing is loaded. Point it over there away from us."

The gun actually did feel good in Willa's hand. She had fired guns before but only at cans and bottles out on the farm. She had never even dreamed of committing armed robbery. She laid the gun next to her on the bed and went back to watching the infomercial.

"Celery, carrots, even zucchini," said the pitchman on TV.

Why would anybody want to juice a zucchini, Willa wondered.

"Alright then." Merle clapped his hands with excitement. "Do we have a plan? In and out of there in less than ten minutes. Move fast. Wallets, jewelry, cash from the registers, that's it. Don't talk to them unless you have to. Meet me up front and we will leave out the main entrance. We'll leave the car running at the curb. Any questions?"

"Yeah," said Willa. "How do you look in prison orange?"

Mack sat in his pickup truck across the street from the motel. He had given up on the binoculars for the night. It was dark now and he couldn't see anything but shadows through the dingy curtain on the second-floor window.

The motel room door opened and two big bastards walked out. They took the stairs down to the parking lot. They opened the trunk of a black Oldsmobile Cutlass Supreme and took out a duffle bag. One of the guys carried the bag back up to the room. Mack watched as the door closed behind them.

"That makes five inside," he said under his breath. "Two big ass rednecks, one slick punk in black boots and leather jacket, a burned-out pillhead greaser, and the girl."

Mack's phone rang.

"Yeah," he said into it.

"Tonight is the night. We want you to take her."

"Well, there is a little problem at the moment."

"What is it?"

"They've got a room full of misfits up there now. One of their guests showed up with a duffle bag full of something. I don't know if it's drugs or guns or cash. Either way, we've got a group of people up there that don't want to be messed with."

"Maybe they'll leave soon."

"Maybe."

"I don't care if they do or don't," the voice changed pitch, sounding erratic and angry. "I want that girl tonight. The private detective from Lexington is putting too much heat on us. We need her as a bargaining chip," he said. "I don't give a shit if you have to kill everyone in that room except her, I want her tonight. You got that?"

Mack exhaled through his nose. He was accustomed to this kind of irrational directive from the boss. "Don't you think we should check with your dad first?" Mack said.

"This is not up to my dad! My dad does not need to make all of the decisions. I have just as much power as he does!" shouted the voice of Montana Jefferson.

"Okay," said Mack.

"Now go up there and get her!" Montana said and then he hung up the phone.

Mack laid the cell phone down. He opened his glovebox and took out a Beretta 92X. He checked the clip and slid it back into the grip. He put his hand on the door handle and pulled it open with a click. The overhead light snapped on as the truck's door began to open.

Before Mack could step out of the truck, the motel room door flung open. Mack quickly shut his truck door and turned off the overhead light. He set the Beretta on the passenger seat and watched as the group of five walked down the stairs. Mack saw a glint of metal as the shotgun barrels caught the motel sign's neon light.

Mack watched the greaser guy get in the driver's seat of a blue Pontiac sedan. The slick dude in the leather jacket took the passenger seat, and the two big rednecks got in back with the girl in the middle.

Mack started his truck. He eased off the curb and fell in behind the Pontiac as it pulled into traffic and turned toward downtown.

22

The hours passed quickly in the bowling alley bar. Cal was having a good time with this country gal from Eastern Kentucky. Who would have guessed it? Maybe he needed to spend more time in her small town.

The bar had filled with people. About a half dozen folks sat on stools at the counter. Most of the tables were also full now. All eyes were focused on the stage at the front of the room. Everyone seemed to be there for the karaoke. They clapped and sang along to the songs.

"You should poke your head out in the bowling alley now," said Penny when she got back to the table from the ladies' room.

Cal cocked his head and narrowed his eyes, trying to understand what she meant.

"Scooch," she said. She waved her hand toward Cal to make him slide around the booth so she could sit back down.

He followed her instruction, still holding his look of curiosity.

"The glow-bowling thing. It just started out there," Penny explained.

"The what thing?" asked Cal.

"Glow-bowling. Black lights and neon and all kinds of craziness. It's fun to watch. It's like being in outer space or something. It just started at ten."

"Ok, you convinced me. I want to see it."

Cal put his hand on Penny's hip to slide her toward the edge of the booth.

Penny dug in her heels and held her ground.

When Cal pushed, his hand slipped across her lap and passed around her waist. Off balance, he tipped forward and suddenly found himself inches from Penny's face with his arms around her.

"Did you plan that?" Cal said quietly. He stared into her eyes.

Penny stared back. "Maybe."

Cal leaned in and kissed her. She turned her face to accept the kiss with her lips. They closed their eyes and embraced, kissing in the shadows of the dimly-lit bar. For a few seconds, the music receded into the background. The people around them faded away.

Cal pulled back slightly, still holding Penny's cheek with his right hand.

"That was nice," Penny said.

"It was." Cal gave her waist another squeeze. "Now let's go see this glow-bowling."

She laughed and got up from the booth. She took Cal's hand as he stood up. "Right through the back hallway by the bathrooms. It leads out to the lanes." She pointed toward the bathrooms.

Cal took one step in that direction when a new song

started on the speakers: the George Jones and Tammy Wynette duet "We Go Together."

"Hang on a second there, cowboy," said Penny. She reached out her hand and grabbed Cal's arm, dragging him back to the table.

The DJ said, "Here's a special request from one of our regulars."

Penny winked at Cal.

He looked at her with terror in his eyes. Surely, she hadn't.

"Penny Fairfax, come on up here," said the DJ. "And bring your new friend. I hear this is his first time on stage."

"This better be a joke," said Cal. His face flushed and he felt sweat start to run down his back.

"Nope," said Penny. "You don't know a soul in here. Come on. It's an easy song. Just read the words along with me."

She took Cal's hand and pulled him toward the stage.

Penny stepped up on the stage like she had done it a hundred times. She took the microphone from the DJ.

"Hey, y'all," she said. "This here is Cal. He's from Lexington, but don't hold it against him."

Cal turned to face the room. He accepted the second microphone the DJ was shoving in his hand. He was so nervous he could barely breathe.

Penny sang her first line. She waited for Cal but he was frozen.

"That's your part," she said into the microphone.

The audience laughed.

Penny gave Cal an elbow in the ribs and smiled. She pointed up at the monitor that displayed the lyrics.

Penny sang her second line and looked at Cal.

He lifted the microphone to his mouth and stammered out the lyric.

Penny smiled broadly and the audience cheered, glad to see this newcomer had gotten the hang of it.

Penny sang the chorus, and Cal joined her, this time with more oomph. He was starting to feel it now. The crowd cheered for them and clapped along. Penny stood by his side, smiling, having fun.

Maybe karaoke wasn't as bad as he thought it would be.

The blue Pontiac pulled up in front of the bowling alley. Luther got out and popped the trunk. He left the car running with the key in the ignition. The rest of the crew exited the vehicle with their weapons concealed at their sides.

"Alright, gang. Let's go make some fuckin' money," said Merle. "Assume the positions. Take as much as you can, and meet back out front in ten minutes."

Randy raised the shotgun to his chest and ran to the right of the building.

Jandy, Luther, and Willa ran to the left.

Merle walked calmly up to the front door. The electric eye registered his motion and the glass door slid open. Music spilled out into the parking lot. The thump of bass pounded in Merle's chest. He raised the shotgun to his waist, pumped it, and walked toward the front counter.

Mack parked his truck a few car lengths back from the Pontiac. He watched as the crew scattered, heading for different entrances. He saw Merle rack the shotgun and walk in the front door.

"Shit," was all Mack said. He opened the driver's door of the Sierra and crouched down behind it. He cocked the Beretta and waited.

Merle strolled up to the front counter casually with the shotgun at his waist. The young clerk behind the desk didn't see the weapon at first.

"Glow-bowling tonight. Twenty an hour for the lane plus shoes. Lemme guess, nine and a half?" The kid had to shout over the sound of the music pumping through the speakers.

"Not bad," said Merle. He leaned on the counter and raised the shotgun. He rested it discretely on the glass top, aimed right at the kid. "Since you're so good with numbers, how bout you count the cash in that register and then put it inside this here pillowcase."

Merle handed the pillowcase across the counter. His motions were slow and deliberate. He drew no attention. He looked nonchalantly from one side of the alley to the other. No sign of Randy or Jandy yet.

Merle was the only person at the counter. None of the other bowling alley patrons had noticed anything out of the ordinary.

The kid froze. "You mean you want me to count the money?" he stammered.

"That was just a little humor for a math nerd such as yourself," said Merle. "You do like humor, don't you," he read the kid's name tag, "Pete?"

"I, uh, yeah. I guess so. What do I do?" asked Pete the cashier nervously.

"This your first robbery?" said Merle.

The kid nodded.

"Ain't that sweet," said Merle. "This here is how it works. You take this pillow case. Take it real nice. No sudden movements." He held out the pillow case again. "Go on, take it. It ain't going to bite you."

Pete took the pillowcase carefully from Merle's hand.

"Good," said Merle. "Now see how easy this is? Okay, next step is you open up that cash register and you take the money out. Then you put it in that pillowcase and hand it back to me. Go on now, let's see you do that."

The kid turned toward the cash register and rung it open. Laser lights spun and flashed all over the counter and across the kid's chest. The white lettering on his t-shirt glowed in the black light. Music thumped in the speakers so loud Merle could barely hear the crashing pins behind him.

"Now don't you do anything stupid, you hear me?" Merle raised his voice to be understood over the pounding beat. "I see you reach for any buttons or make any signals to one of your pin monkey buddies, I'll put three holes in your chest and roll you down the lanes." He tapped the barrel of the shotgun to remind the kid it was there.

Pete began filling the pillow case with cash.

"That's real good, Pete. Real good." Merle looked toward lane 20 and saw the exit door on the end swing open. Randy walked in and headed straight for the last lane at the end of the alley.

Merle watched Randy open his shirt to reveal the shotgun and then hold out the pillowcase to the first person he came to.

The family in the lane stopped. The dad was mid-roll when his wife motioned for him to return to the seats.

They glanced around with terror in their eyes, looking for someone to help them. But the commotion of the glow-bowling made it impossible for those in the next lane to recognize what was happening.

"Atta boy, Randy," said Merle. He looked to the opposite door in lane 1. Still no sign of the third team.

"Goddamn junkies," said Merle. "Where are they?"

Outside the door of lane 1, Jandy, Luther, and Willa crouched in the bushes. Jandy was becoming frantic. Moaning to the other two to indicate his desire to proceed. He kept looking at his partners and then wildly at the door.

Luther and Willa were doing their best to ignore his moaning and gesturing.

"I can't!" said Willa. "I don't think I have the nerve. I can't go through with it."

"You're holding the gun and Merle is already in there robbing the place," said Luther. "There's no turning back now. A few minutes and we're home free with the cash."

"Let's just do one more line before we go in," said Willa. "To help with the nerves."

"We don't have time for that!" shouted Luther. He stood up and racked the shotgun. "Afterward you can have as many as you want."

Jandy had worked himself into a frenzy. When Luther stood up it was all the signal Jandy needed. He shoved past them, almost knocking Willa down as he kicked the door open and stormed inside.

"If you don't come in here you're not getting a penny of the score," said Luther to Willa. He glared at her for a second and then followed Jandy inside.

Willa gripped the SIG Sauer in her right hand. She strained her ears toward the road, listening for sirens in the distance. She heard nothing but the dull thumping of bass from the music inside. She pushed the door open and went in.

As soon as Merle saw Jandy enter the door, he breathed a sigh of relief. "Bout damn time," he said to himself. "Easy there, tiger, keep a low profile," he said when Jandy stomped up to lane 1 and raised the shotgun level with a college kid's face.

The kid's eyes opened wide in horror. Merle could see the teen's reaction from his vantage point at the front desk ten lanes away.

Jandy thrust his pillowcase into the center of the group at lane 1. They got the idea and began filling it with their wallets and purses.

Merle smiled and turned back to his own business at hand. "Hey, Pete. How you doing over there?" he said. "You see those big 300-pound rednecks working their way toward the center of the alley?" He didn't wait to see if Pete was looking. "Those are my boys. You see, we're taking this place for every penny you got. Now you just remember our arrangement, okay?"

"Arrangement?" Pete said nervously.

"The one about how you don't do anything stupid and I don't put you in the grave before you have a chance to pop your cherry," said Merle. "You ever been laid, Pete? No man wants to die before he has a chance to get laid."

"No," said Pete.

Merle laughed. "Say, I kind of like you, Pete. Maybe

after this is all over we get you laid. I got some girls be glad to help a guy like you out."

Pete swallowed hard. He had no idea what this crazy man was talking about. The only two things he knew for sure were he didn't want to die, virgin or otherwise, and two, he did not want to see this maniac ever again.

Merle shifted his eyes between Randy, Jandy, and Pete. Randy and Jandy were steadily making their way to the center of the lanes. The plan was working perfectly. A few more minutes and they would be gone with the score.

Out of the corner of his eye, Merle spotted Luther sneaking along the wall, trying to blend in with the shadows around him. Merle watched him open the door that led to the bar. Willa was right behind him.

"Listen up! Everybody get on the ground!" shouted Luther. He raised the shotgun as he walked toward the stage.

The music in the bar was so loud almost no one heard him. A few people turned to see what the commotion was about. They froze when they spotted the two armed robbers.

A man and a woman were on stage singing a George Jones duet. Luther headed straight for them. He hopped up on stage and snatched the microphone out of the woman's hand. He repeated his threat into the microphone. "Get on the ground now. All of you."

This time his voice cut clearly across the P.A. system. He racked the shotgun with his other hand.

The DJ cut the music inside the bar. Gasps echoed throughout the dark room.

The thump of bass continued to pound in the bowling alley just beyond the walls of the bar. It was the only sound in the room other than Luther's barked orders.

"Wallets, watches, and purses," said Luther. "That's what we want. My lovely associate will be walking around the room collecting. Keep your faces to the ground. Hand up your valuables as she passes. We don't want to hurt any of you. Don't make us. This here shotgun is real and it will blow a real hole in the head of anyone who tries to get brave."

Luther dropped the microphone on the stage with a thud. He shouted at a few of the patrons who remained seated. "Face down. Now!" Motioning with the shotgun as he spoke.

Luther turned toward Willa for the first time since entering the bar. He realized she had hardly moved. Only a step inside the door.

"Get!" he shouted at her.

Willa sprang into motion, carrying her pillowcase from one table to the next. She carried the SIG Sauer in her left hand. Paralyzed with fear, she barely even felt the gun in her hand, almost forgot she was holding it.

"Thank you," Willa repeated each time someone placed an item in her pillowcase. Like she was selling girl scout cookies at the grocery store. Thank you for your business. Come again.

Luther headed for the bar. He shoved the shotgun in the bartender's face. "Empty the register right now. Do it!"

The bartender did as she was told. She lifted stacks of cash from the tray and laid them on the bar.

Luther had never seen so much money in one place. He snatched at the bills and stuffed them in his pockets.

*   *   *

Cal and Penny knelt on the stage with their faces pressed to the wood floor. The microphones they held just moments ago were now discarded in front of them, one still rolling from where Luther had dropped it.

"I take it this is not part of the act?" whispered Cal.

"No," said Penny, "I can't think of any karaoke song with a robbery interlude."

"Folsom Prison Blues?" said Cal.

"As long as we aren't the 'man in Reno'," said Penny.

Cal smiled slightly. "Let's just give them the money and hope they get out of here fast," he said. "It's not like they are going to shoot every one of us. There are at least forty people in here."

Cal watched the woman's low-top Chuck Taylors as she made her way through the crowd. Bare legs stepping around chairs and dodging tables. Her thin arm held the pillowcase outstretched.

When she got to the stage, Cal reached into his back pocket and removed his wallet. He leaned back so he could place the wallet in the woman's bag. Just enough so he could see her face in the dimly-lit room. He froze, wallet in hand, staring up at her.

Willa shifted her eyes around the room, visibly uncomfortable. "Put it in the bag, man."

Cal didn't move. "I know you," he said.

"No, you don't, dude," she said. "Hey, lady, put your rings in, too." Willa shook the bag toward Penny.

"Yes, I do. You're Willa Taylor," said Cal.

Willa's eyes widened. For a moment, she looked like she might cry. Drop the gun and forget the whole thing. Run out of the room in shame. Then she quickly pulled it together.

"I don't know no Willa. You got the wrong gal, mister. Now quit talking before I have to shoot you. I know how to use this thing." She nodded at the pistol in her left hand.

Cal slowly put his wallet in the bag. He didn't take his eyes off of Willa. He was sure now. It was her. After all, he had spent the past few nights sleeping in her room at the trailer.

"Willa, don't do this. We can fix it," said Cal. But she was out of earshot, on to the next table.

"You want to tell me what is going on?" whispered Penny.

Cal sat back on his haunches. Recognizing Willa had shaken something loose in him. Like he was no longer afraid. "That's the girl," he said. "The one I have been looking for."

"No way," said Penny.

Cal didn't respond. He watched as Willa hit the last table. She walked over to the bar where Luther was stuffing the bills in his pockets. What he couldn't fit, he dumped into Willa's pillowcase.

By the time Willa and Luther reached the door that led back to the bowling alley, Cal was already on his feet. "I have to stop her," he told Penny. "I have to do something."

Cal broke into a run toward the door that Willa had just exited.

Penny followed close on his heels.

Mack waited in the parking lot with his Beretta drawn. He listened for sirens or any indication the police had been called. All he heard was the dull rhythmic music coming from inside the bowling alley. His orders were to take the girl tonight. That's what he was going to do. He watched the door, held his breath, and waited for what would happen next.

When Cal pulled open the bar door, the loud music hit him like a wall of sound. Laser lights spun all around him. He became disoriented, had trouble getting his bearings. When his eyes slowly adjusted to the visual onslaught of the glow-bowling, he spotted Willa by the front desk.

Cal crept toward the front desk. He felt Penny right behind him. He knew it was dangerous for both of them, but it was too late to stop.

As Cal approached the desk, he counted four robbers total. Willa and the other guy from the bar had been joined by a guy in a leather jacket waving a shotgun at the teenage front desk clerk, and another big dude with a beard who walked up from the opposite direction.

Cal instinctively reached under his jacket, his fingers feeling for the .38 semi-automatic pistol that would normally be holstered under his left arm. They came up empty. Of course, he had left the weapon in the MG for date night. One of the only times he wasn't packing.

"What do we do?" said Penny. She and Cal were only ten feet from the front desk.

"Hold it right there," said Cal. He shouted to be heard over the music.

Merle and Luther turned to see who had spoken. They saw Cal standing nearby squared up like he was ready to fight them.

Merle laughed. "Is this a joke? Are you going to challenge us to a bare-knuckle brawl?"

"I'll do what I have to," said Cal.

"Now, mister, you are making a serious mistake," said Merle. "We're about ten seconds away from leaving this joint without a single dead body in our wake. I know you don't want us to break that streak."

Randy slowly raised his shotgun until it was aimed at Cal.

Merle made no movement.

Cal kept his eyes on Merle.

"You see we have you outnumbered," said Merle. "And in case you haven't noticed, we have guns. Are you stupid or something?"

Cal didn't move.

"Now, we are going to back our way right on out of here, and you are going to let us do that. Got it?" Merle raised his eyebrows as he asked Cal the question.

"You may have me outnumbered, but you won't get away with this crazy plan. The police are on their way," Cal lied. "Correct me if I'm wrong, but I have you pegged as the boss of this crew."

Merle smiled. He seemed flattered, as though Cal had just given him a compliment. In an instant, his smile turned to a flash of anger. "Would somebody please turn off this godforsaken music?" he shouted at the teenage desk clerk. "I can't even hear myself think and the fucking BeeGees ain't helping."

The kid fumbled with the stereo controls until he found the switch to cut the music. The bowling alley went silent, but the laser lights continued flashing.

In one motion, the crowd of bowlers turned toward the

front of the room. They now all understood exactly what was happening.

"Thank you. That's much better," said Merle. His voice sounded painfully loud and awkward in the newfound silence of the large room. He adjusted his tone and continued, "Now, friend, back to business. Like I said, it's time for us to go. We got everything we came for."

"Let's go. The cops are coming!" said Luther.

"Hold your horses there, old chap," Merle said to Luther. "We've got a vigilante on our hands. Let's deal with one thing at a time."

Luther shut up, but he began pacing by the desk. Visibly upset and agitated.

Merle ignored Luther's fidgeting and turned back to Cal. "My associate is right, friend," Merle said, still looking directly at Cal. "Time for us to split."

"I'm not a cop and I don't even care what your end game is," said Cal. "As far as I'm concerned what you took is yours if you can get out that door alive. Even my wallet. Keep it. But I need the girl." He nodded at Willa.

Merle looked confused. "You know this guy?" Merle asked Willa.

Her ears still rung from the music that had abruptly ended. She looked at Cal again, trying to remember him. How did he know her? What did he want with her?

"No," she said.

"What's he want you for?" said Merle.

"Hell if I know."

"It seems the lady doesn't know you, pal. And I ain't running no prostitution ring."

"I know her family and—" Cal said, but before he could finish, he felt the cold steel of a pistol pressed against the side of his head. Heavy breathing and excited moaning sounds accompanied the hard barrel of the weapon.

Merle smiled. "You missed one," he said.

Jandy's moaning escalated, proud of himself for catching Cal off guard.

"Good boy," said Merle to Jandy. "Now put him on the ground and come over here with your brother."

Cal lowered his fists.

Jandy kicked Cal's legs and shoved him forward violently.

Cal stumbled. He landed facedown and skidded across the thin carpet, feeling the rug burn across his cheek. Cal felt Jandy step over him as he lay prostrate on the carpet.

After a few seconds, Cal raised his head, but all he saw was the crew of robbers running toward the sliding glass exit. The automatic doors opened in front of them. In seconds they would be gone, and with them, his hope of catching Willa.

Mack watched the doors slide open. He tensed the muscles in his shoulder and crouched down behind the open door of his pickup truck. The barrel of the Beretta stuck out from the crack between the door frame and the truck body.

The two big guys came out first. They stopped just outside the door and scanned the parking lot, looking for police. The guys were so intent on searching for red and blue lights that they missed Mack's pistol aimed right at them only about thirty feet away.

The lookouts signaled all clear, and, moments later, the other three robbers exited the bowling alley.

"Hey, you there!" Mack yelled.

The party froze.

"Right over here. You see my piece sticking out from the truck?" said Mack.

"It's the cops," said Luther. He made a move like he was about to run.

"No, it's not," said Merle. "Just hold still."

Merle took a step toward Mack. "Listen here, pal. I have had about all the interruptions I can handle tonight. Now, if you haven't noticed, we just pulled a job in this here bowling alley, and we're about to go count our cash. I'm going to give you three seconds to get in your truck and drive away before we open fire on your ass."

"I wouldn't do that if I were you," said Mack. "I ain't the cops and I don't want your money. I just came for the girl."

"The girl? What the hell is going on tonight?" said Merle, exasperated. "Are you with the other guy?"

"What other guy?" said Mack, still crouched down behind his truck door.

"The other guy inside who wanted to take this broad with him. What's she got, a golden snatch or something? Why's everybody want her?"

Mack didn't respond.

Merle looked at Willa. "How bout this one? You know him?"

Willa shook her head.

"I've got half a mind to let you take her," said Merle. "She's getting to be a pain in my ass. And, besides, I prefer the idea of splitting the jack four ways instead of five."

"You can't do that," said Luther. "I would get her cut if she doesn't."

"The hell you would. Nobody is getting my cut but me," said Willa.

"Well, we'll split it though, right, honey? Like we talked about. You and me," said Luther to Willa. He paused for a second, the gears in his head turning slowly as he formulated a new plan. "Maybe you should go with this guy and let me take care of the money. You know, we could meet later and split it up." He was trying to talk sweet to her, convince her. "I mean seeing as how this guy won't let us leave until you go with him. Maybe you should for now." He reached for Willa, waving his arm as though to guide her toward Mack's truck.

Willa raised the SIG Sauer and aimed it at Luther. "Don't you touch me," she said.

"Oh, you're gonna shoot me? Is that how we're playing it?" said Luther.

"You're the one about to turn me over to some stranger with a gun!" Willa shouted back.

"Fuckin' junkies," muttered Merle. He turned back to Mack. "How bout I give you a two-for-one deal? Take the girl and her deadbeat boyfriend. I'll even throw in a wad of cash from this here pillowcase."

Mack didn't respond. He watched the group of thieves, waiting.

"I thought we were in this together?" said Luther to Merle. He was whining, like his feelings were hurt.

"I'm sure you would do the same to me," Merle said. As he spoke he reached in the pillowcase and removed a wad of cash. He held it out toward Mack. "What do you say, pal, let's make a deal. Do me a favor and get rid of these two. I'll make it worth your while."

"The hell with that!" Luther shouted. He raised his

pistol and cocked it. He aimed it at Merle. "I got a better idea. You give all that cash to me right now."

As soon as Luther raised the weapon and threatened Merle, Randy and Jandy swung their shotguns from Mack to Luther.

Mack stayed silent, glad to have the heat off of him for the moment. He watched as Luther became increasingly erratic, swinging his pistol back and forth between Merle and the two goons while they all argued about who was leaving with the cash. The big guys kept their shotguns steadily aimed at Luther.

"Now you've done it," said Merle, still using his confident, calm Southern drawl. "The cops will be here any minute and I'm not going down like this. Luther, put your fuckin' gun away before you get shot. Give me those bags of cash. I don't care what you do with Willa, but I'm leaving right now."

Merle reached for the pillowcase in Willa's hand.

Luther swung his pistol toward Merle.

Randy could no longer restrain himself. He pulled the trigger on his shotgun and blew Luther halfway across the entryway.

Luther's body ricocheted off a large, concrete pillar. He stumbled and fell backward into the parking lot.

Luther rolled over and sat up, shouting in pain. He covered his stomach with his left hand, trying to stop the bleeding. With his right hand, he raised the pistol and shot Randy in the leg.

Randy dropped to the pavement. His shotgun skittered across the sidewalk through the open sliding door.

At the sight of his brother's shooting, Jandy screamed his awful moaning shriek and pulled the trigger on his own shotgun. The discharge blasted a concrete planter to pieces next to Mack's truck door. Shrapnel scattered across the entryway and cascaded onto Mack's hood. A second shot from Jandy finished Luther where he lay, awkwardly slumped against the exploded planter. His lifeless fingers still gripped his pistol.

Jandy threw down his weapon and ran over to his brother. Randy lay on the concrete bleeding. Jandy stood there holding his brother's head, moaning and wailing as the sliding doors opened and closed again, slamming against Randy's thick legs.

For a split second, Merle raised the shotgun and considered returning fire. But he couldn't decide what to shoot at. Luther was dead. Randy and Jandy were out of commission. Willa had dropped her pistol. She was crouched in the parking lot covering her head and screaming. Mack had not even fired a single shot at him or anyone else.

Merle watched as Mack slowly lowered his Beretta. He, too, lowered his weapon. Both men wanted something different. Neither had any intention of impeding the other's access to what he wanted.

Merle grabbed the two pillowcases dropped by Willa and Luther. Cash spilled on the sidewalk as he lifted them. He took one last glance at Randy and Jandy. Those two could fend for themselves. Sticking around meant getting busted for armed robbery and probably murder. No way he was taking that chance. Merle hoisted the bags on his shoulder and took off running down the street.

Mack didn't waste any time. He advanced on the scene with the Beretta raised in front of him. He was crouched over but moving quickly. When he got to Willa, he grabbed her by the arm and pulled her toward the truck.

It was like Willa suddenly awakened from a dream. As soon as Mack's hand gripped her forearm, she started screaming again. The SIG Sauer lay on the ground nearby, but she didn't have time to grab it.

Mack wrapped his arm around her waist and started dragging her back to the truck. One arm around the girl, one arm raised, pointing the Beretta in the direction that Merle had run just in case he resurfaced.

Mack shoved Willa into the open driver's door of the truck. He pushed her across the bench to the passenger's side and got in after her. He immediately revved the engine and peeled out of the covered entryway, swerving to avoid Luther's body that was slumped over in the middle of the road.

Cal watched the whole thing go down from inside the bowling alley. He had started to follow Willa, but stopped as soon as the gunfire began. Each time the sliding doors slammed on Randy's legs, they bounced back open to reveal more carnage. Cal watched helplessly as two men were shot before his eyes. He watched as Willa, who had been so close to his grasp, was abducted by another strange man and carried off in a GMC Sierra pickup truck.

The second Mack's truck pulled out, Cal resumed the chase. He ran into the parking lot.

Two men lay on the ground bleeding. One of the big guys held the other big guy in his arms, rocking him rhythmically back and forth. The fourth man, the slick guy in the leather jacket, was running down the street. He appeared to be carrying all of the pillowcases full of cash.

Cal hopped over the side of his MG, not wasting time with opening the convertible's door. He fired up the engine. Just before he gunned it, Penny swung a leg over the passenger side. Her boot dangled in the air until it came to rest on the floorboard. She quickly pulled in the other leg and plopped down in the seat beside Cal.

"You should wait here," said Cal. "This is going to be dangerous."

"Are you kidding me?" said Penny. "Did I mention I got the babysitter for the whole night?"

Cal shrugged. "The whole night, eh? Better buckle up then." He slammed the car in gear. They zipped out of the parking lot in pursuit of the pickup truck that carried Willa and her captor.

23

Mack drove the truck with his right hand on the wheel. His left hand held the Beretta in his lap, aimed at Willa in the passenger seat. He had not said a word since they left the bowling alley.

"At least tell me where we're going," pleaded Willa.

Mack drove on in the dark, silent.

They passed through the last stoplight in town and continued out into the countryside. Darkness closed in around them as the town lights faded in the rearview.

Willa reached for a crumpled cigarette pack on the dashboard. She picked it up and shook out a Camel Light, watching to see if Mack would have any reaction.

He stared forward, unflinching.

Willa pushed in the truck's cigarette lighter and waited for it to pop, holding the cigarette between her teeth. She wasn't much of a smoker, but at least it was something to do. It gave her a sense of control and helped take her mind off the circumstances.

The cigarette lighter popped out and she withdrew the

glowing hot cylinder. For a second she considered using it as a weapon. Hold it on the guy's face and make him wreck. The Beretta in his hand made her think otherwise. She raised the lighter to her cigarette and lit it. She exhaled smoke in the truck.

Mack cracked the passenger window with the automatic switch on his door. It was the first time he gave any acknowledgement of Willa's presence.

Willa looked at Mack as she exhaled the cigarette smoke. She saw a man about fifty years old. Short hair, strong arms and chest, reasonably thin waist. In good shape for his age. He wore a tight short-sleeve shirt with a collar and a few buttons in front. Willa noticed a tattoo on Mack's thick, tan forearm.

"Were you in the army or something?" she asked.

He glanced over at her as he drove. "Or something," he said.

Willa was relieved to hear the man finally speak. She figured she had a better chance of surviving whatever was about to happen if she could get him to open up a little.

"Navy?" she asked.

Mack grunted in affirmation.

"What'd you do? Shoot people?"

Mack turned to face Willa. He squinted his eyes. "Give me one of those," he said.

Willa took a Camel Light out of the pack. She lit it off the end of her own cigarette and handed it to Mack.

He leaned forward and opened his mouth slightly.

Cautiously, she placed the filter end of the cigarette in his mouth. Mack took a drag and exhaled.

"I spent time on a ship called the U.S.S. *Harlan County.* You ever heard of it?"

"No," said Willa. "You mean like the county here in Eastern Kentucky?" She was joking, trying to lighten the mood.

To Willa's surprise, Mack answered, "Yes. The ship was named after the county."

"Oh, now I know you're full of shit," said Willa.

"I'm not. Look it up," said Mack. He took another drag from the cigarette.

"Why would the Navy name a big boat after a small county in Kentucky?"

"You'll have to ask them about that."

"You mean you were on that boat while you were in the Navy, and then you ended up living right here in Harlan County, Kentucky when you got out?" said Willa.

"Ship," Mack corrected her. "And yes."

"Did you go out on the ocean?"

"I did."

"I've never been to the ocean," said Willa. "What's it like?"

"You mean the beach or the ocean?"

"Either I guess."

"They are different places. The beach is where you go for spring break to get drunk. It's a fun place," said Mack. "The ocean is not the beach. It's unforgiving and brutal. It's not a fun place. It's work, hard work. It's a place of survival."

"Were you in a war?"

"You ask a lot of questions, don't you?"

"I don't know. Just passing the time I guess. You never told me where we're going."

"I wasn't in a war anyone has heard of. We did missions. Lots of construction work on the water."

"Where?"

"Lebanon for a while. And then Cuba."

"That's cool. I want to go to Cuba," said Willa.

The two fell silent for a while. They drove further into the darkness of the country road.

Willa wondered where they were going, what would happen to her. She thought about Luther and the other guys. Was Luther dead? Did Merle get away? Does he have her money?

After a few minutes, she said, "If you were in the Navy, that means you're a good person, right? You aren't going to kill me or rape me or anything, are you?"

"Being in the Navy doesn't necessarily make me a good person," said Mack.

Willa put her hand out the window. She felt the cool, night air blow across the little hairs on her forearm. She heard the crickets and cicadas humming in the wilderness around them.

"But are you though?" she said.

"Am I what?" said Mack.

"A good person."

Mack didn't respond right away. He thought about it for a few moments.

"I used to think so," he finally said. He rolled down his window and tossed out the cigarette.

"I think you are a good person," said Willa. "I don't think you want to hurt me."

"There's a difference between wanting and doing," said Mack.

"But you can always make a choice," said Willa.

"I'm not so sure about that these days," said Mack. He relaxed the Beretta in his lap. He turned and glanced out the window to his left. "I look around this town. I see the people who live here. The poverty, the drugs, the desperation. And I wonder what choice there is anymore. How does a man make an honest living in times like these?"

"No one has to do bad things. They decide to," said Willa.

"The world presses down on you so hard. You get to feeling like you can't breathe. You get to feeling like you have no other options other than to take the one opportunity left. The one that's right in front of you holding a wad of cash, telling you everything's going to be fine."

"You can always leave," said Willa. "We can leave right now. We can drive to Lexington. We can drive to California. We can go anywhere we want."

Mack didn't respond.

"You don't have to do this. Whatever it is we're doing," said Willa.

Mack stayed silent.

"Will you tell me your name?"

Willa was grasping at straws, trying desperately to get Mack to see her as a person. Anything she could do to convince him to let her go.

"I don't think that's a good idea," said Mack.

Willa remembered from some crime show that her best bet was to humanize herself, make the killer walk in her shoes and understand she had thoughts and feelings.

"My name's Willa Taylor," she blurted out. "I live with my parents in the Sunshine Trailer Park. I'm nineteen years old. I want to go to college at the University of Kentucky. Have you ever been to Lexington?"

"I have."

"That's good. I want to go there. I can leave right now. Just leave town and never come back. If you let me out of the truck. You can just pull over here."

"I bet you could."

"Where are you taking me?" said Willa, her voice sounding more frantic now. "What are you going to do to me?"

The pickup truck continued on into the night.

Cal and Penny were lucky on the way out of town when another car took the same road they were traveling. The car stayed between them and the pickup truck, even when they passed through the final stoplight and left the city lights. Cal kept the MG a few hundred yards back on the country road with the other car shielding them from Mack's GMC truck. The presence of another car on the lonely road made it less obvious that the front car was being followed.

"Where do you think they're going?" asked Penny after they had been driving in the darkness for about ten minutes.

"I don't know. You tell me," said Cal. "Is there anything out this way?"

"Hmm…not that I can think of. Just lots of quiet country."

Penny leaned back in the convertible. Her hair swirled in the wind.

The lights of the town were gone. Far away from the light pollution of the city, the stars shone brightly in the night sky.

"Look up there," said Penny with her head tilted back. "That's why I love living in the country."

Cal took his eyes off the road and looked above them as he drove.

"It's beautiful," he said. He reached over and put his hand on Penny's leg.

"You know what that one's called? Up there with the four corners and the three across the middle?" said Penny. She pointed into the sky.

"What?" said Cal.

"Orion. Do you know his story?"

"You mean like the myth about the constellation or whatever?"

"Yeah. He was a hunter who loved a woman. But the woman's father didn't like him so he blinded Orion."

"Oh yeah? That's a nice story," said Cal.

Penny laughed. "It gets better though because his sight was restored by a god named Helios. His vision came back with the rising sun of morning."

"So he was blinded and then got his sight back."

"That's the way I heard it," said Penny.

"What's the moral of the story then?" said Cal.

"The moral?"

"Yeah, you know, like what are we supposed to learn from it. It's Greek mythology, right? Doesn't it stand for something or tell some kind of parable?"

"I'm not sure that's how it works," said Penny.

Cal thought for a moment. "Let's see, this guy likes a woman," he said. "He wants her and he pursues her, he'll do anything to have her."

"Uh huh."

"But then her dad comes along and decides this Orion

guy isn't worthy of his daughter. He thinks she can do better and he doesn't like the way Orion is looking at his little girl."

"So he blinds him," said Penny.

"That's right. He blinds him. He figures that's that. He's taught this character a lesson. Nobody messes with his daughter unless he approves of it."

"But?" said Penny.

"But this other guy—or god, did you say it was a god?" Cal looked over at Penny.

"Helios, the god of the sun."

"Right, the god of the sun. He intervenes, says he thinks maybe Orion got a raw deal. All Orion wanted was to date this lady. But her dad messed him over and wrecked his chances. So Helios steps in and restores Orion's sight, gives him another chance. Did I miss anything?"

"I think you summed it up pretty well," said Penny.

"Okay then. So the moral of the story is go after what you want. It might be hard, and you might face some challenges, but in the end, if your intentions are pure, things will work out."

"You got all that from one little line of Greek mythology?"

Cal smiled. "I mean, really all those stories are interpreted from the eye of the beholder, right? You see what you want to see."

Penny nodded.

"I guess that's what I wanted to see," said Cal.

He looked at the night sky again. He tried to pick out the constellation Penny had referred to.

"Those four corners up there are him, huh?"

"Yep."

"Alright then."

They drove quietly for a few minutes, the summer air blowing through their hair. The dense smell of wild nature pressed in around them. Grassy and mossy and floral.

Up ahead, the truck's tail lights flashed red. The driver was braking, about to make a turn. The car in front of Cal also slowed, causing Cal to tap his brakes.

Cal and Penny watched as the pickup truck carrying Willa made a right turn into a gravel driveway.

As the truck turned, the car in front of them sped up and passed the truck. Their buffer vehicle was gone.

"There's no way we can make that turn without him knowing we're following," said Cal.

Cal slowed down as much as possible. They passed the gravel driveway on their right and cruised up the country road. Behind them, they saw the truck's tail lights disappear around a bend.

"Oh yeah, of course!" said Penny. "I know where we are now."

"Where?" said Cal.

"This is the old coal processing plant. I'm not even sure if it's still operational. I don't think anyone has worked out here in months, if not years."

"Up that gravel road?" said Cal.

"Yeah, maybe a quarter mile at the most. Not too far. That has to be where they are going."

"Okay, then I guess that's where we're going, too," said Cal. He killed his headlights and pulled the MG off on the shoulder just down the road from the gravel driveway.

"We are?" said Penny.

"You're the one who said you wanted an adventure. Remember, I asked you to stay at the bowling alley."

"Oh please. This is the most fun I've had in years," said Penny. She was already halfway out the door before she finished her sentence.

Cal opened the glovebox and took out his .38. He slid it in his empty shoulder holster and trotted after Penny.

"Do you know where you're going?" he asked her when they reached the gravel road.

Penny whirled around to face Cal. "To save that girl," she said. She proceeded up the path with the sound of gravel crunching beneath her boots.

The coal processing plant looked like an abandoned attraction at Disney World with all of its conveyor belts and cranes and exposed gears and levers. Ivy grew up the sides, winding in among the bricks, forcing them apart. Its searching tendrils swallowed the building whole, slowly digesting it from the outside, leaving the bricks crumbling and broken. Rusted iron gates marked the entrance of the grounds. One side of the gates hung open. Fresh ruts were cut in the gravel from the truck's wheels as it entered the grounds ahead of Cal and Penny.

As they crept up to the gates, they could see the place was abandoned, but it was not empty tonight. Someone lurked inside the dilapidated warehouse. A light from inside spilled out on the property through the broken windows, illuminating the grounds in an eery glow.

"Look," whispered Penny.

Cal followed her pointing finger. He saw the pickup truck parked near a metal door marked RECEIVING. The truck was empty.

They crouched in silence by the iron gates, straining to

hear something, anything. They could hear no sound but their own soft breathing.

Blind from the hood Mack had placed over her head, Willa had no idea where she was or where they were going.

Mack held her arm, guiding her as they walked over the uneven ground. Below her she could see her feet, the low-top Chuck Taylors, stepping over and stumbling on debris from the crumbling building. She felt Mack's hand on her left arm. He gently pulled her one way or the other to avoid the obstacles in her path. Light from the beam of his flashlight occasionally flicked across her field of vision and illuminated the area around her legs.

"What is this place?" she asked, her voice muffled through the hood.

"You'll see."

Willa heard a steel door open in front of her and then Mack's voice told her to step up and walk through the doorway.

Willa sensed danger. She panicked and began thrashing around, trying to wrench herself free of Mack's grip.

"Help! Somebody help me!" she shouted.

Her voice echoed against the walls of the building. Her cry for help reached the surrounding hills and returned to her, unanswered.

"There's nobody around here for miles," said Mack.

Willa stopped shouting. She did as she was told and entered the building.

Once inside, the floor became smooth. A light above her lit the concrete floor on which she stood. The floor was covered with a thin layer of black dust that wafted into the air around her shoes with each step.

Mack led Willa further into the building.

She could tell from the echoing sound of their footsteps that they were in a large room, maybe a warehouse of some kind.

Mack stopped walking. He tugged Willa's arm so she would know to stop.

"Put out your hands," said Mack.

She did. She felt the back of a chair directly in front of her.

"Sit down."

"I don't want to," said Willa.

"Sit down and I'll take that hood off," said Mack.

She patted the back of the chair and groped downward, feeling the contour of the seat. Her hands gripped the sides of the chair and she lowered herself onto it.

The air in the room was dusty. She could feel the small particles of dust in her lungs when she breathed. Her nostrils, already clogged from snorting the pills, could barely draw air.

"I can't breathe in this thing," she said.

She felt Mack's hand on her head. He gripped the top of the hood and pulled it off. Static electricity plastered her hair to her face. She reached up and smoothed it out.

The chair where she sat was the only piece of furniture in the cavernous warehouse. Huge pieces of industrial equipment lined the perimeter of the room. Conveyer belts, chutes, cisterns, massive machines connected to hydraulic presses.

Willa and Mack stood alone in the giant room. A fluorescent light overhead lit the space, casting long shadows into the corners.

"What is this place?" said Willa. Her voice resounded against the concrete walls.

"This is the old coal processing plant. It's where they used to bring freshly-mined coal to get it ready to ship out to the world," said Mack.

"Good to know. I could use a few lumps of coal, but it doesn't look like it's open today. Maybe we should try again tomorrow," said Willa.

"This place has been closed since they launched the new prep plant down the road," said Mack. "But we aren't here for the coal."

"What are we here for?" said Willa.

"Somebody wants to meet you," said Mack.

Willa swallowed. "Who?"

"Actually we've already met," said a voice from the shadows.

Willa turned to face the voice. She waited for the speaker to reveal himself.

Out from the darkness stepped Montana Jefferson.

Willa immediately recognized the long hair, the jeans, and the woven poncho.

"Hey, you're the guy from The Farm," she said. "The drug-free counselor guy."

"You are half right," said Montana. He began walking toward Mack and Willa. His bare feet, noiseless on the concrete floor, were caked with coal dust.

"Why are you here?" said Willa. "Screw that, why am I here?"

Montana stopped a few feet from Willa's chair.

"You are my good luck charm. My leverage," said Montana.

"Your what?"

Montana smiled. "It seems we have a mutual acquaintance. A man who is investigating us both. A man who doesn't belong here, and who needs to leave town tonight, one way or another. And you, my dear, are going to help me convince him to do it."

Willa had no idea what Montana was talking about. She had not seen him since her brief stint at The Farm. She wondered if maybe he was holding a grudge against her for giving up on his drug treatment plan.

"Look, man, I'm sorry about leaving The Farm," she said. "Is that what this is about? The place just wasn't for me."

Montana laughed and then grew serious in an instant. "Little girl, I don't give a shit if you get clean or OD on your pills. What you do is your business. The problem is your parents do care and so does this guy they hired to find you. And now your problem is becoming my problem."

Willa thought back to the bowling alley. It seemed like a lifetime ago when she watched Luther get shot even though it had only been about an hour. She remembered the first guy who had tried to stop them—the one from the karaoke bar—and it dawned on her what Montana was talking about.

"You mean that dude from the bowling alley? I don't even know him," she said.

"Yes, that dude from the bowling alley," said Montana. "And it doesn't matter whether you know him or not. He knows you. He has been looking for you." Montana paused to let his words sink in before continuing. "And he is about to find you. Any minute now I presume. Don't worry, you will have plenty of time to get acquainted."

Montana raised his voice so it echoed loudly around the

empty processing plant, "Tyson! That's your queue! Are you here yet? I know you followed them. I have eyes everywhere in this town. Where are you? Come on out and let's have a chat! Maybe we can make a deal. If you cooperate I might let the girl walk."

Cal and Penny were crouched in the bushes outside of the coal plant. They heard Montana's shout and exchanged a nervous glance.

Light spilled out through the open doorway and sliced across the debris-strewn path between the building and their hiding place.

"So much for the element of surprise," Cal whispered.

Cal could see into the warehouse, but he could not see the chair where Willa sat, nor could he see Montana, but he recognized the smug hippie's voice. He motioned for Penny to stay behind. "Take the MG and go get help." He tossed her the keys.

Penny looked at him with pleading eyes. She knew Cal was right. Why expose them both if Montana only knew about one of them? She touched Cal's forearm and then watched as he stood up from behind the bushes and stepped into the slice of light.

Cal entered the room through the open door. He saw Willa, and then he saw Mack and Montana standing behind her. Mack held the Beretta at his side.

"United at last," said Montana. His voice boomed across the concrete floor. "You finally found her, Tyson."

Montana applauded sarcastically as Cal closed the distance between them.

Cal remained silent as he approached. He surveyed the

room, searching for any other henchmen who might be hiding in the shadows.

"Ain't she a peach," said Montana. He patted Willa on the shoulder.

Willa shook his hand off her shoulder and scowled at the floor.

"Now you've got her," said Montana. "What do you want to do with her?" He dragged out the last sentence slowly. His eyes crept down Willa's neck to her waist and down her tan legs.

Mack held his Beretta on Cal as he patted him down. He found the .38, along with Cal's cell phone. He took them both and slipped them in his pocket.

"I knew you were trouble," said Cal to Montana. "Did your daddy give you this warehouse, too? Your own personal torture chamber?"

Montana stared at Cal. "I see you've been doing your research," he said.

"What the heck is going on here?" said Willa. "I barely know any of you. Typical men, talking about me like I'm not even here. I'm not your prize or your pet or whatever you guys think I am."

"Why don't you tell her why she's here?" said Montana to Cal.

"Look, Montana, I think you got the wrong idea somewhere along the way," said Cal. "I came here as a favor to Elroy Taylor. You may know him. He's a former employee of your father's."

Willa's head dropped when she heard her dad's name.

Cal continued, "Elroy asked me to help him find his daughter. He and Debra were worried. So I drove down from Lexington and, what do you know, I found her. End of story. Now let me take her back home and I will leave town. You will never see me again."

"Hey, I told you I don't need saving!" said Willa. "I'm a grown woman. I don't have to do anything I don't want to do. Elroy isn't the boss of me any more than you two assholes are. Now if y'all want to stay here and compare your peckers, be my guest, but I'm leaving!"

She started to stand up, but Montana pressed her back into the chair. "What's the rush?" he said. "We're just getting to know each other."

Willa rolled her eyes and groaned.

Cal shifted his weight from one foot to the other. "Is there any reason your man here needs to hold his weapon in such a threatening manner?" He nodded at Mack.

"He's fine for now. Don't worry about him," said Montana. He took a step back and resumed the smug hippie affectation he had used toward Cal at The Farm. "You see, when an outsider such as yourself comes poking around in our business, people get to talking. It disrupts our way of life. Questions start getting asked, the media starts to get nosey. It can cause a lot of problems for a small town economy such as ours."

"I think you mean it can cause problems for those at the top of the food chain, the people who are pulling the strings," said Cal.

Montana closed his eyes. He pivoted to face the walls of the warehouse. He raised an arm and pointed at the equipment surrounding them. "Millions and millions of dollars," he said. "That's what an operation like this costs. That's what it takes to build a business like this one. Millions, hundreds of millions. Billions even. This equipment—take that coal crusher there." He pointed at the giant slab and the hydraulic press connected to it. "That single piece of equipment costs a small fortune."

Cal listened to Montana ramble.

"Do you have any idea what an infusion of one hundred million dollars does for a small town economy?" said Montana. "How many jobs it creates? How many mouths it feeds?" He paused, waiting for an answer but he got none. "My family built this town. Fucking built it. We made it. This town would not exist without us. Are you aware of that?"

"Even if that were true, you think that gives you the right to do anything you want?" said Cal.

"Pretty much. Yes, I believe I do," said Montana. "And it means I will do whatever it takes to keep some outsider from destroying what we have. Whatever it takes."

Before Cal could respond, he heard a noise outside the building that sounded like footsteps sliding on gravel. Cal cursed under his breath, guessing who was out there and what was about to happen.

At the sound, Montana froze. He motioned for Mack to go check it out.

Mack, who had been standing stoic and silent behind Willa, raised the Beretta. He quickly reached the door. He placed a shoulder on the wall and then slowly peeked around the corner with the pistol raised in front of him.

Cal, Montana, and Willa watched as Mack disappeared out the door. Within seconds, they heard a woman's voice shouting in protest. Mack reappeared leading Penny into the warehouse.

Cal's spirit sank when he saw her.

"The more the merrier," shouted Montana. "Bring her over here."

They watched as Mack led Penny over to the chair where Willa sat.

"And who do we have here?" said Montana.

Penny raised her eyes to meet Montana's. When he saw her, his expression changed. "Hold on, I know you. I remember you," he said.

"I can't believe I trusted you," said Penny.

"That's right. Miss Penny. You spent some time with us at The Farm a few years ago, didn't you?" said Montana.

Cal could see that Montana still held some sort of charismatic effect on Penny. She dropped her eyes and dragged her boot in the coal dust.

"I did," she said. "Still sober, too." She mumbled it, as though she wasn't sure of herself.

The confidence Cal had seen earlier in the night from Penny was gone when she faced the man who led the cult from which she had escaped.

"Well, now, how about that? See, Tyson, we're not all bad," said Montana. "Got you a sober little gal to play with. And if I remember right, she's a real wildcat in the bed."

"That's enough of that," said Cal. "What's your plan here exactly? I think you're in over your head."

"No, I don't think so. I think my head's right where I want it to be," said Montana. "In fact,"—he reached in the pocket of his poncho and withdrew a small plastic baggie —"I believe I'll have a little taste just to keep my head where it is."

Montana dipped a finger into the baggie and withdrew a fingernail full of white powder. He raised it to his nostril and sniffed. Then he repeated the process in the other nostril. When he finished, he held out the bag to Willa and Penny. "How bout a little blow, ladies?"

The women stared at the floor, disgusted at the realization that Montana was exactly the opposite of the wholesome drug-free counselor he pretended to be.

Montana shrugged. "Suit yourself." He tucked the baggie back in his poncho.

"Here's the problem, Cal, old buddy old pal," said Montana. "Now you know too much. That's the thing about cocaine. God, I love it. But it really gets me talking. I just run on and on, and here I went and told you more than I should have. And these ladies, they've heard it all, too." Montana looked at Penny and Willa. "Now what are we going to do about that, Mack? What are we going to do?"

Mack didn't respond. He was used to his boss asking questions that had no answer. He knew it was best to let the theatrics run their course.

Montana surveyed the room as he thought.

"Montana, there's no need to do anything stupid," said Cal. "The three of us can get in my car and head right on out of here. So far you haven't committed any real crimes." Cal knew that wasn't true, but he was trying to keep Montana calm. Better if he didn't do anything to rile him up.

The coked-up killer turned Cal's suggestion over in his mind.

"I'm not sure you're right about that, Tyson. All three of you, you know me now. You know too much about me. I could never relax again as long as you are out there in the world knowing my secrets."

The gravity of the situation began to sink in for Penny and Willa. Montana Jefferson was going to kill them.

"Let us go!" shouted Willa. She stood up to run. This time Montana swung his arm, slapping her face with his open hand. She fell back to the chair. Blood trickled from the side of her mouth down her chin.

Cal flinched, knowing there was nothing he could do with Mack's pistol aimed at him.

Montana gathered himself again. He wiped off his hand, straightened his poncho. "Mack, does this equipment still work?" he asked.

Mack shrugged. "Hasn't been turned on in years."

"Mack," Willa whispered under her breath. She made a mental note of his name, remembering how she had asked it before and been denied.

Montana walked over to the control panel that powered the machinery. He raised the plastic cover and studied the controls. After a few seconds he reached down and flipped a switch. The conveyer belt came to life with the sound of grinding metal.

The conveyer belt surrounded the perimeter of the factory. Its gears churned and spun throughout the room. The noise was deafening. Montana had to shout in order to be heard.

"Good old American engineering!" he yelled over his shoulder, turning to smile at the group.

Montana flipped another switch and the hydraulic press for the coal crusher engaged. At the end of the conveyer belt the crusher's massive jaws began spinning. They looked like two giant steamrollers with spikes on them. Between the two rollers was a 6-inch gap where small chunks of coal passed once they had been crushed by the powerful jaws.

Montana rejoined the group, leaving the machinery running behind him.

"Mack, it's a damn shame, isn't it?" said Montana, raising his voice over the noise.

Mack hesitated. He waited for Montana to continue.

"Yes, indeed. A damn shame," said Montana again.

"What's that, sir?" said Mack.

"How we get these pillheads who break into places and try to steal from us. They break in one night thinking they'll have a thrill in the old coal refinery. Then maybe they'll steal some scrap metal and take it to the junkyard, get some more drug money," said Montana, shaking his head. "Damn shame. This equipment is dangerous. Nothing to play around with. They ought not to be in here. Playing around in that coal car on the conveyer belt. All drugged up like they are. They might get confused and accidentally lock themselves in it. And that coal car, why it just does its job, takes its load right above the crusher and dumps it into the jaws below. Yessir, those pillheads would never be seen again. Crushed to tiny pieces and dumped down the chute into the slurry pond. Damn shame."

Montana took the Beretta from Mack. He waved the pistol at the trio of prisoners and motioned for them to walk toward the conveyer belt. When they reached the machinery, Montana reached up and opened the lid of one of the coal cars. "Get in," he said.

"What if we don't?" said Cal.

"Then I'll shoot you right here."

"Do what he says," said Cal to the women.

"But Cal!" said Penny.

Cal figured he would rather face the coal crusher than a bullet in the head. At least they would have a few more minutes to figure something out. Maybe the police would miraculously arrive. He stepped into the coal car.

He could see the bottom of the car had a hinge that ran lengthwise. The hinge was fastened to the side of the car by a large, metal clip. If the clip were retracted, the hinge would swing and the floor of the car would drop out below him, dumping him out the bottom.

"You next," said Montana.

Penny and Willa both stepped into the car with Cal.

Montana closed the lid.

The three occupants had to kneel in the car to fit once the lid was closed. They heard it latch and lock in place.

After locking the lid to the coal car, Montana returned to the control panel that operated the machinery. Using a joystick, he maneuvered a long metal arm over the steel car. At the end of the arm was a giant magnet. Montana lowered the arm until it clicked in place with a whooshing magnetic snap. When he raised the arm, the coal car raised with it. The steel enclosure lurched upward and swung freely in the air. The inhabitants of the car gasped in unison.

Montana rotated the arm and positioned the coal car about three inches above the moving conveyer belt. He disengaged the magnet and the car dropped onto the conveyor belt. It began moving slowly down the line toward the coal crusher where it would eventually drop its load into the powerful jaws below. The conveyor belt creaked and groaned under the weight, but it moved steadily along. The coal car began its slow journey about one hundred yards from the crusher.

"The world is about to lose two pillheads and a meddling detective!" shouted Montana. "And we'll be better off for it!"

Montana turned to go. He nodded at Mack and handed the Beretta back to him.

"Make sure they reach their final destination, old boy!"

Montana said. He patted Mack on the shoulder and left the group alone in the processing plant.

24

Cal, Penny, and Willa huddled together in the cramped coal car. The space was tight and dark. Coal dust filled the air, making it hard for them to breathe. Only a tiny crack of light shone from the seams where the hinge held the trap door closed. The light was just bright enough for Cal to make out the terrified features on the women's faces. His own face looked no different.

"What are we going to do?" said Penny. "We'll be crushed to pieces!"

"Maybe the police will come. Surely someone called them at the bowling alley after the shootout. They can't be far behind us," said Cal, but he did not feel confident.

"You heard them," Penny said. "No one around here for miles."

Cal kneeled and tried to peer out of the tiny seam in the metal. It was no use. He couldn't see anything. He pressed the lid. Threw his shoulder at it, but the latch held solid.

The churning gears of the conveyor belt droned below

them. They felt the car jostling as it rolled down the line. The deafening grind from the coal crusher grew ever louder.

"Maybe if we brace ourselves in here," Cal said as he pressed his feet and his back against opposite sides of the steel car. He wedged himself in place and lifted his butt off the floor of the car. "See, like this," he said, imploring the women to try it.

Willa didn't even look at Cal. She sat silently with her back resting against the car. "It's no use," she said. Her voice sounded calm amid the raucous, as though she had resigned to her fate. "Even if we could wedge ourselves, how long do you think we could hold that pose once the bottom drops out?"

"We at least have to try!" said Penny. She pressed her boots against the wall of the car like Cal had demonstrated.

"It's just prolonging the inevitable," said Willa.

"All we need to do is hold on long enough. If we can just figure out a way to hang in there until help arrives."

"And then what?" said Willa. "So we dodge one of life's bullets. The next bullet will come right behind it. What's the use in trying anymore? It's a never-ending onslaught."

"That's the drugs talking," Penny said. "Believe me, I've been there. I know the despair and depression, and the overwhelming desire to give up. You have to push through it."

After a few moments of silence Willa said, "Maybe so." She did not seem convinced.

The jaws of the coal crusher slammed together, shaking the conveyor belt and rattling the rails on which the car rode.

Willa spoke again. "I have been around coal since I was

born. I've seen my dad operate this equipment. I probably even came to this very place when I was a kid." She pounded a fist against the side of the metal car. It echoed in the small space. "That coal crusher, it's unstoppable. It takes everything that comes at it, and it always wins. Once you get caught in its jaws, it will crush you into tiny pieces and dump you out in the river with the rest of the waste."

Willa's eyes flashed in the dim light. Her face was calm and tired.

Cal opened his mouth to speak but he didn't know what to say. He had no words of encouragement to offer, no advice to give.

"The slurry," Willa continued, "all the chemicals and the mud and the shit and the waste that comes out of this refinery. They take what they want, and then they dump the rest. Whatever they spit out the other end—the watery, sloppy mess of unwanted trash—that's the slurry," she said. She closed her eyes, bowed her head till her chin touched her chest. "It's what is left after they've used up the good parts, squeezed out all the life they can squeeze. That's the slurry, and that's what we are about to become," she mumbled.

Cal lowered his body back to the floor of the coal car. He pulled his knees up to his chest and wrapped his arms around them. He understood Willa's point. He felt it, too, sometimes. The never-ending barrage, the weight of life pressing down, the futility of trying. How no matter what you do, it is somehow never good enough. The feeling that life takes all you have to give until you have nothing, and all you are left with is the crap. In a few moments he wouldn't feel anything ever again, and maybe that was okay. Just resign, give in, embrace the slurry.

The conveyor belt rattled and shook as it approached the coal crusher. The force of the snapping jaws vibrated across the floor of the coal car. Cal felt it deep inside his body. The end was near. Less than a minute now.

Penny was also calm, knowing there was nothing more she could do. She raised her eyes to meet Cal's and somehow managed to smile.

"Why didn't you leave when you had the chance?" Cal asked Penny. "You could be long gone by now, home with your daughter."

"I guess I should have. I just couldn't leave you two. I thought maybe if I…oh, I don't know what I thought. I guess I just wanted to help, but look where it got me."

"No sense dwelling on it now," said Cal. "Let's try to stay positive. We still have some time."

Through the crack in the hinge, they saw the grinding coal crusher appear below them. The coal car rolled slowly out on the rails above the crusher. In seconds, the hinge would drop and the bottom would swing out, dumping them into the waiting jaws.

Penny put her arm around Willa and hugged her.

"Help!" Cal shouted. He banged his fists on the metal walls. "Is anyone out there? Help us please!"

Willa remembered the man who had abducted her. Mack. Was he still out there? Could he hear them? He was their only hope. She pleaded with him through the thick steel enclosure.

"Mack, I know you're out there. Remember how I said you're not a bad person? You can help us. This is your chance to do the right thing again. You *do* have a choice. You *can* change. We all can. We always can." Willa seemed to be pleading as much with herself as she was with Mack.

"Don't let us die in here," she shouted. "Please help!"

Even with the noise from the machinery, Mack heard Willa's cries for help. He stood next to the conveyor belt where Montana had left him. He watched the coal car slowly roll toward the crusher.

This was not the first time Mack had been asked to commit murder for the Jefferson family. Over the years his employer had forced him to do heinous things to earn his paycheck. The strikebreaking, the surveillance, the kidnapping, the lying, even murder. Mack had gotten used to it over time. He was only doing what he had to do.

He listened to the trio pleading for their lives inside the coal car, knowing this would be one more crime in a lifetime of crimes. Why should it be any different?

But it was different. Somehow this young woman meant more to him. Killing a criminal—a grown man—that didn't bother him as much. But this innocent teenager, maybe that was a step too far. Maybe he would not be able to forget it like he could the others. Maybe this act would weigh on his conscience forever, the one that would finally break him beyond the point of no return.

How did he get to this point in life? The point where another man, an evil man, controlled his actions. The point where Mack could no longer make a decision for himself. He was a Yes Man to a twisted crime boss. Montana was a disgusting, hateful person who had no respect for Mack or anyone else.

Maybe it was time for a change. He remembered Willa's words about how he could go anywhere. Just start over from scratch.

The coal car was nearing the end of the line. It would reach the crusher soon. The trio would be dead in a matter of seconds if he didn't do something.

Mack reached up and gripped the lever. His hand shook as he pulled the lever down hard. The noise from the gears whirred and then faded out. The machinery began powering down. Mack stepped back and released the lever. He pressed a button on the control panel, and the latch on the coal car unlocked.

Mack took two more steps backward. He moved slowly, in a daze, almost stumbling. What had he done? He had defied his boss. And Montana Jefferson was no ordinary boss. Mack knew far too much about the Jefferson operation. Montana would never trust him again. By saving Willa, Mack had put his own life in danger. He knew he had to leave. Get out of town tonight and never look back. Montana would be searching for him.

Despite Mack's trepidation, for the first time in years, he also had a strange sense of relief. He could go anywhere, do anything. He could start over. He could make a new life.

Mack turned and ran through the open door of the warehouse. He climbed in his truck without looking back. He drove into the night and disappeared.

The sound of screeching metal like brakes on a train ripped through the warehouse. The crushing jaw slowed its grinding motion and stopped pounding.

The latch on the car popped open. The machine's whirring noise faded as the equipment powered down.

Cal's ears rang in the sudden silence. He, Penny, and

Willa stared at each other, stunned.

"What happened?" whispered Penny.

"I don't know," said Cal.

"Did it break?" she said.

Cal raised his head over the top of the coal car. The room appeared to be empty and silent. Cal swept the building and saw nothing.

"It was Mack," said Willa. "I know it was him. He saved us."

"I don't see him anywhere. There's no one here," said Cal. "Whatever it was, I sure am glad for it."

Cal stepped off the coal crusher and helped the ladies down. Coal dust covered their bodies from head to toe. Cal did his best to wipe the dust from his face and hands. He watched as Penny brushed the dust from Willa, carefully working to reveal the blonde hair underneath.

Willa's eyes were tired and weary. She stood still, subdued, and allowed Penny to brush her face clean like a mother wipes chocolate ice cream from the chin of her child.

"That was close," Cal said.

There wasn't much else to say. The group would never know the act of mercy bestowed on them by Mack Abbott or the decision he made to change his life that night.

The three walked to the MG in stunned silence.

At the car, Penny took her cell phone out of her purse and called the police. They stood in the gravel driveway, filled with gratitude and relief, and waited for the police to arrive.

* * *

It was six in the morning by the time Cal, Penny, and Willa had briefed the police and gotten clearance to leave the scene.

The police released Willa on two conditions. First, she had to testify against Merle and his crew for their part in the bowling alley robbery. Willa had no problem agreeing to that.

The second condition was a little more strange. She could not mention any details about Montana Jefferson or Mack or any of the events that transpired that night at the coal refinery.

The police assured them they would look into the case and investigate all parties. They wanted Willa, Cal, and Penny to keep quiet about it unless they were told otherwise. Anxious to get clear of any criminal charges for her part in the robbery, Willa signed her statement without any questions.

But Cal's suspicions got the better of him. Why would the police be so careful to silence any news about Montana Jefferson or the coal refinery? The agreement they offered to Willa was almost certainly designed to keep the Jefferson Mining Company out of the headlines, Cal thought. Maybe he was being overly cynical. He hoped he was wrong.

"Can we get my car later?" said Penny once they had reunited Willa with her parents back at the Sunshine Trailer Park. "I'm exhausted and I just want to go home."

Cal nodded in agreement. He was exhausted, too. He hoped maybe he could take a shower at Penny's place, wash off the coal dust that still covered his skin. "Do you happen to have a spare couch I can crash on for a few hours?"

Penny looked at him and smiled. "I think we can figure something out," she said.

They drove in silence for a few minutes with the wind blowing through their hair. The cool mountain air soothed their skin, refreshed their spirits, cleansed their bodies and their minds from the events of the previous night.

Voices on the local radio station quietly murmured the morning news. Penny cocked her head to listen.

"Hey, are they talking about us?" she said. She reached for the dial and turned up the volume. It was the voice of Riley J. Jefferson.

Jefferson: "Rest assured, Jefferson Mining Company had nothing to do with the events that transpired at our old refinery last night. This was the work of a group of low-life druggies. They broke into our facility and did a considerable amount of damage to our equipment. We thank God no one was hurt."

Reporter: "Mr. Jefferson, is there any truth to the rumor that this incident was connected to a robbery at the bowling alley earlier Saturday night?"

Jefferson: "Well, now, that will be for the police to investigate and determine. We have complete faith in our chief, and we know he will do the right thing and bring these hoodlums to justice."

Reporter: "What about reports that your son, Montana Jefferson, is somehow involved?"

Jefferson: "My son, well, hmm, my son has had his challenges in the past. I won't pretend that isn't true. He's a good boy and he has turned his life around. I'll say again, we believe the events of last night were the work of vandals and drug addicts. None of the Jefferson family authorized nor participated in whatever mischief took place at the facility."

More reporters clambered to ask questions, each one talking over the others. Without wasting a moment, Riley Jefferson quickly pivoted the conversation.

Jefferson: "Now, while we're all here, I would like to take this opportunity to make a big announcement. Jefferson Mining Company is officially opening a new hydraulic fracking facility right here in Eastern Kentucky next year. We expect this new plant will create at least three hundred jobs, and it will be our sincere goal to fill as many of those positions with folks right here in our hometown!"

As he listened, Cal shook his head slowly.

Jefferson: "Let's end this interview right there on a happy note. I know all of you have a Sunday morning church service to attend soon. I'll be there myself, and I haven't even had my breakfast yet. Thank you and have a blessed day."

Cal turned the radio off. Penny dozed with her head on his shoulder.

Cal didn't blame her. They had heard enough.

25

Two weeks later, Cal was on his way back to Harlan County for another visit. He wanted to check on Willa and her family. And another thing: there was a certain country gal he wanted to see again, too.

Penny stood on her front porch, smiling and waving as Cal pulled in her driveway. Even prettier than he remembered.

After a happy reunion, they went to visit Willa. She had checked into a drug rehabilitation center the day after their adventure at the coal processing plant. Willa had decided to get clean and get her life back on track.

It was a sunny day in late August. Puffy, white clouds floated in the blue sky above the convertible as they drove along the rural road.

Cal glanced over at Penny when they pulled up in front of the New Day Appalachian Rehabilitation Center.

She had a curious look in her eyes.

"What?" he said.

"Nothing. Just looking at you."

"It seems like you want to say something."

"I've been trying to decide whether to bring this up or not," said Penny.

"Well, now you have to."

Penny smiled. "You remember that night on the way to the coal refinery?"

"How could I ever forget it?"

"I know what you mean. But, seriously, remember the stars above us, how pretty they were?"

Cal remembered it well. "Yes, I do. You taught me about the constellation, Orion."

Penny hesitated. "Exactly. We talked about the moral of the story."

Cal nodded. He parked the car and turned off the engine.

Penny continued, "Later on, I read more about the myth. There's more to it. You know how we said it was a happy ending because Helios gave Orion his sight back?"

"I remember," said Cal.

"I wanted to tell you the rest of the story. How after he gets his sight back, he decides to go hunting. That's how he got his nickname, Orion the Hunter."

"Okay," said Cal.

"He goes hunting and he vows to kill everything in the forest. Then Gaea, the goddess of the Earth, hears about his plan to slaughter her animals. So she sends a scorpion and the scorpion kills Orion first."

"So he dies?" asked Cal.

Penny nodded.

"I guess the moral isn't what we thought then," said

Cal.

"I agree. Both times Orion wanted something that he couldn't have. He reached beyond his grasp and he tried to take more than his share. And eventually he got what was coming to him."

"Wow, that's kind of heavy," said Cal.

"Yeah. I'm thinking the moral is something like 'don't be greedy, don't want more than your share,'" said Penny.

"Be happy with what you have or you might end up losing everything."

Penny smiled at Cal. "That's how I read it, too."

"Well, I'm glad we got that settled," Cal said. He patted Penny's leg playfully. "Are you trying to tell me something?"

"Maybe."

"I'll keep that in mind then."

"Hey," Penny said.

"Yes ma'am?"

"Let's do another night drive and look at stars soon."

"I'm in. But maybe under different circumstances this time!"

The facility was a nice, clean place in a modern building with professional staff—nothing at all like the so-called rehabilitation center at The Farm.

They found Willa sitting in a courtyard in the center of the building. The courtyard was about the size of a tennis court, open at the roof to let in the sunshine. The grounds were landscaped with lush greenery. A trickling fountain fed into a small koi pond in the center of the courtyard. A couple of tables and sparse chairs had been placed around the space for patients and guests to sit and chat.

"There she is," said Cal when he spotted Willa by the koi pond.

Willa looked up at the sound of Cal's voice. She saw Cal and Penny, and she smiled broadly at them. Her face looked completely different than it had two weeks before. She looked hopeful and happy.

"Hi there," she said as Cal and Penny approached.

"You look great," said Penny. "I can see it in your eyes."

"I think I just got a good night's sleep for once," Willa said, shrugging off the compliment. "And I'm getting some sun out here in this courtyard all day."

"How's it going so far?" asked Cal.

"Well, two weeks down," said Willa. "So I guess that's a start."

"I'm so happy for you," said Penny. She leaned over and hugged Willa in her chair. "You are doing so good."

"Yeah, they say the first couple weeks are the hardest."

"It's true. I remember," said Penny.

"So you really have been through this, too?" Willa asked.

"I sure have. Three years sober now. And I'm never looking back. It gets easier and easier. It really does."

"That's what I keep hearing, but it sure doesn't feel that way," said Willa.

"Listen, if there is anything I can do to help, I want you to let me know, okay?" said Penny.

"Okay."

"I mean it. Do you hear me?" Penny said, using a friendly but serious tone. "I've been there. I know what it's like. It's hard work and you will have days where you think you can't make it."

Willa didn't respond at first. She watched the orange

fish swimming in the koi pond. After a few seconds, she said, "You mean like as a sponsor or something?"

Penny smiled, her eyes full of compassion.

"Yes," said Penny.

"I think, um, I think I would like that," said Willa. "If you don't mind."

"I would be honored," said Penny.

The three sat quietly, watching the fish dance in the water. The fountain trickled in the background. The bright sun warmed their skin.

Willa broke the silence. Looking at Cal, she said, "What happened, did you decide to stick around for a while? I thought you were a city boy."

Cal laughed. "Something about those country girls I guess. What can I say?" He grinned at Penny.

"Yeah, we are pretty great, aren't we?" said Willa.

"Yes, we are," answered Penny. "And speaking of us country folks, I distinctly remember you asking where you could get your own pair of cowboy boots," she said to Cal, giving him a goodnatured poke in the ribs.

"Did I?"

"You most certainly did," said Penny.

"You know, I think I would look good in a pair of cowboy boots," said Cal. "What do you think?" he asked Willa.

"I think I'll stick with my Chuck Taylors," she said, rolling her eyes.

"Well, we better get going on that today. I know just the place," said Penny.

"What's the rush?" asked Cal.

"We need to hurry if we're going to have you ready in time for karaoke tonight."

Cal's eyes widened with terror. "Oh no, not again," he said.

"You know you love it," said Penny. "And just wait till you hear what song I picked out for us!"

About the Author

Josh Boldt writes crime fiction and mystery novels set in the American South. He is the author of two novels: *The False Favorite* and *Slurry*. His fiction explores the darker sides of human nature and vice, and contains elements of classic hard-boiled noir; however, Boldt's stories cover contemporary issues. He holds an M.A. in English from Eastern Kentucky University. He lives in Lexington, Kentucky. The next novel is currently underway. Visit joshboldt.com for news and updates.

www.ingramcontent.com/pod-product-compliance
Lightning Source LLC
Chambersburg PA
CBHW021114110726

47900CB00007B/2183